STO

**DO NOT REMOVE
CARDS FROM POCKET**

BATHING UGLY

A RICHARD JACKSON BOOK

BATHING UGLY

REBECCA BUSSELLE

ORCHARD BOOKS
A division of Franklin Watts, Inc. / *New York*

ORCHARD BOOKS
387 Park Avenue South
New York, New York 10016
ORCHARD BOOKS CANADA
20 Torbay Road
Markham, Ontario 23P 1G6
Orchard Books is a division of Franklin Watts, Inc.

MANUFACTURED IN THE UNITED STATES OF AMERICA
Book design by Tere LoPrete

10 9 8 7 6 5 4 3 2 1

The text of this book is set in 11 pt. Baskerville.

Library of Congress Cataloging-in-Publication Data

Busselle, Rebecca, 1941–
    Bathing ugly / Rebecca Busselle.
    p. cm.
    "A Richard Jackson book."
    Summary: Chosen to compete in the camp's bathing ugly contest
because of her weight, Betsy decides to push the idea to its limit
and force the campers to rethink their ideas about the importance of
outward appearance.
    ISBN 0-531-05801-8.   ISBN 0-531-08401-9 (lib. bdg.)
    [1. Beauty, Personal—Fiction. 2. Contests—Fiction. 3. Camps—
Fiction. 4. Weight control—Fiction.] I. Title.
PZ7.B9664Bat 1988
[Fic]—dc19   88-17929
                                                           CIP
                                                            AC

✷ Contents

BATHING UGLY

1 ✻ *Goodbye Old Life*

Every summer, my friends left the heat and boredom of St. Louis and went to camp. Every winter, when it was camp sign-up time, I begged Mother to let me go. She said she and Daddy liked having me around in the summer, and to remember all the fun barbecues we'd had. She reminded me that I could use the months to improve my reading. She argued that I was too young.

Finally she gave in because I had only one friend left in the city—Isabel, whose father owned a limestone quarry by the river. Isabel and I would go to work with her father and spend hours hanging over the chalky cliffs, watching men set up dynamite charges. When the whistle sounded for blasting, we'd run to her father's office and wait for the explosion. After the all clear we'd take a swim in the deep, jade-green crater. Though Isabel's father assured Mother I was perfectly safe, I knew she was horrified by my days at the quarry. When I began saving my allowance for a hard hat and talking about blasting caps, it was too much for Mother. "This is it," she announced. "Next summer you'll be thirteen. You are going to camp, young lady."

That's how on a sultry June day I found myself wedged between my parents in a crowded airport terminal, on my way to Camp Sunny Days for ten magnificent weeks.

"It's going to be a glorious summer, Sweetie," Mother said, swiping my bangs from my eyes. "No electricity, no phones, just good traditional values. Those places are hard to find, so hard to find. The kind of camp I went to when I was a child."

Indeed it was hard to find a camp like Sunny Days. Most kids went to specialty camps: One of my friends went to basketball camp, where she was drilled by a seven-foot coach all day and watched videos of the team at night. Another spent two months in front of a monitor and keyboard at computer camp. My richest friend skied in July. However, I couldn't play the cello, so music camp was out, and I had no confidence tennis camp could improve my backhand. Strangely enough, the solution came through my neighbor, Louise. Thanks to her mother, who had the same old-fashioned ideas as mine, I was being sent to camp Sunny Days—the last obscure outpost of pre-civilization.

Still, it was away.

An ocherish-green light of heat and jet exhaust hung over the terminal, making the inside of my nose feel peppery—though maybe I felt that way because I had to say goodbye to these parents I'd so wanted to be free of. I was afraid I might sneeze, but out would come big sobs I wouldn't be able to stop. How could that be? I'd been waiting years for this moment.

"Here we are, Tootsie Roll, your big send-off day," Daddy said heartily as he pulled at my ear lobe.

"Don't call me Tootsie Roll, Daddy." I batted his hand away, though what I really wanted to do was hold it. It always felt so big and comforting around my own. If we hadn't been standing at the ticket counter with other St. Louis Sunny Days campers, that's just what I'd have done—if Daddy would have let me. I was tall as his chin now, and I sensed my size was connected to the way he'd begun to treat me. The week before when I'd slipped my hand into his, he'd taken it out and linked it through his crooked arm the way he did Mother's. "Allow me to escort you," he'd said.

Now that I'd checked in and gotten a window seat in no-smoking, we began to make our way across the crowded terminal to the security check, where the metal detector beckoned like McDonald's golden arches. Outside, a jet roared its take-off, muffled by the huge, quivering, glass window. A family pushed by us, one little kid dragging a plastic doll by the foot, while its head mopped the floor. A baby was screaming.

"Why's this place so noisy and crowded?" I demanded crankily.

Mother laughed that odd way she does when she's nervous, a ha-ha-ha-ha that starts high on the scale and jumps down. "Nothing to be alarmed about, dear. All airports are noisy." She was trying to reassure me, I knew, but her laugh made me jumpy.

"Don't forget I've never been on an airplane before." I crumpled a wad of my skirt into my fist.

"How I wish one could still travel on decent trains, with Pullmans and porters," she sighed. "It was the last civilized means of conveyance. All the gracious things of life are passing."

"I know, Mother. And no one has any manners anymore, right?"

Daddy hadn't been paying a bit of attention to me. He was peering around the arched dome of the airport like a tourist in New York City. Now his head came out of the clouds. "Betsy, that sarcasm is quite unnecessary. Please apologize to your mother."

"Sorry, Mother," I said, truly regretful, and kissed her cheek. Even though Daddy automatically took her side, I knew this time he was right; there was no point antagonizing her right before I went away for ten weeks. It's just that I was so tired of hearing how the world was going downhill, how clothes were poorly made and you couldn't get decent help and no one did things properly anymore.

Mother is the most old-fashioned person I've ever met. She admits it too; in fact she's always saying she was born in the wrong century. She should have been a Victorian, she says, and it's easy for me to imagine her with a bustle and parasol. She does all she can to keep that image—high-necked blouses with ruffles around her throat and short jackets that emphasize her tiny waist—a waist so small I've seriously wondered if she had a lower rib removed, the way some women did at the turn of the century. Mother's hair is long, with streaks of gray, and she wears it in a bun on top of her head. When she sleeps, she plaits it in a loose braid, like someone out of *Little Women.*

To take me to the airport she wore a royal-blue linen suit and the usual high-necked blouse. On her head she wore a hat, an honest-to-God hat with a pheasant feather. She must have been roasting— though like all true Victorians she never sweats but merely glows.

"Mother!" I'd screeched when I saw her done up that way. "Why on earth are you wearing all those clothes? It's hot out there, Mother. The snow melted last winter."

"One always dresses properly for travel."

"But I'm the one that's going away, not you. I suppose you want me to deck myself out like that?"

"Of course not, Dear Heart," she'd said serenely. "I know you don't share my feeling for appropriateness."

I cut my eyes at the other Sunny Days campers in line for the security check, and saw it was time to say goodbye. Some girls were clinging to their mothers as though this was goodbye forever instead of ten weeks; others looked as though they'd practiced goodbye a hundred times, smacking the air with big, wide kisses and rolling their fingers in a wave.

I turned to Daddy first. My cheek pressed into the softness of his neck under his smooth-shaved chin. He's always well shaved, no matter what time of day. Even on weekends he never has stubble or that bluish look some men get. And he's always perfectly dressed too. He wears the same dark suit every day—there are three exactly alike in his closet—but on weekends he wears gray slacks, a cashmere pullover, and his loafers. The only time he ever steps out of character is on Christmas Day. Then instead of dark gray socks he wears one green sock and one red sock. Every year he waits for my grandmother or one of my aunts to comment on this, and then he says, "Well you see, I have another pair exactly like them at home!" And he roars.

" 'Bye Daddy. Thanks for leaving the office early to take me to the airport."

"Hey there, Dumpling. No appointment is more important than getting my Sugar off to camp, you know that."

We locked our baby fingers together and squeezed hard. It was a secret signal we'd always had, one even Mother didn't know. *We're together and everything is all right.* I knew I'd miss him so much—maybe not miss his dinner-table talk of meetings and investments and clients, but miss something that came from locked fingers.

Mother held my head between her hands, her gloved fingers pressing gently on my cheeks. She studied my face—not critically as she sometimes did— but as though looking for something lost. Although campers might be watching, I hugged her so hard she tilted backward.

Daddy steadied her. "Whoa Dumpling! Down girl! You're getting pretty big to be all over Mother."

I felt my face grow hot. Why did he need to say things like that? To make it worse he laughed. I decided I'd try not to think of Mother and Daddy again, just concentrate on what was ahead: a line of Sunny Days campers—all girls who'd be with me for the summer. Ahead were all the mysteries of who they were and how I'd fit in with them.

The parents stood aside in a group watching their darlings line up for our new, independent lives. All the parents, that is, but Mother.

From the corner of my eye I saw Mother leave Daddy's side. I looked squarely over at her, as she marched determinedly around the airport. My airport. She spotted a stewardess hurrying toward the security check, trailing a wheeled suitcase behind her like a little dog. Mother's white-gloved hand stopped her like a traffic cop.

She'd done it, really done it. I could have prevented this if only I'd been stronger a week ago, if I'd argued more.

"Sweetie," she'd said, "when you go off to camp I'm going to get a stewardess to keep a special eye on you."

"What's this about? I don't need anything special, Mother."

"Your grandmother did it for me. Always. I'd go alone during spring vacation to visit my aunt, and she'd go on the train first and tip the porter."

"Why? Didn't she trust you?"

"The point is you're a young girl traveling alone."

"Mother, come off it. This is the eighties—the nineteen-eighties, not the eighteen-eighties. I'm only flying two hours to Minneapolis. And there'll be lots of kids."

"Kids. Exactly. You need a special eye," she clucked.

I stood helpless, counting seconds—one Mississippi, two Mississippi—as she talked to the stewardess. I clutched my purse against my chest. Eye—what was this special eye? I closed my eyes and hoped the world would be erased. I prayed none of the other campers knew what was going on, especially Louise who, I was sure, felt a little funny having me at her camp. One idea came in a loop, tight and driven as a bicycle chain: Oh please let me be like the other campers please please let me be like the other campers please please.

Mother's white finger pointed over the line of girls. To me. The stewardess nodded a bored, polite nod. Mother stood there making sure she knew just which girl was different and should receive her special eye.

My face was hot deep into my skull as I imagined how Mother described me as she pointed. "That one, yes," I imagined her chuckling, "behind the blonde. See her? The stocky one with short, straight, brown hair."

I glowered down at my shoes, those new flats with grosgrain bows I'd been so proud of just a few hours ago. But when I looked up, the stewardess had vanished and Mother had linked her arm in Daddy's, looking smug, while Daddy rocked back on his heels, hands fingering the change in his pockets.

I felt my parents' eyes on me as I put my purse and gym bag on the conveyer belt, but there was no way I'd look at them again. As I stepped through the metal detector, I relented enough to give my hand a careless flip over my shoulder, which they could interpret as waving or brushing off a bug.

2 ✳ A Special Eye

I looked out the jet window as the plane taxied to the runway, certain I'd made a grave mistake. A room this big wasn't supposed to fly. The wheels should stay on the ground where they belonged. The cabin lights blinked nervously, and cold air roared at my face through a little blower. I'd buckled my seat belt the instant I sat down, with my dress twisted and mashed under my legs. I gave it a tug. "How very becoming," Mother had said when we bought it. "Diagonal stripes do wonders." As I pulled at the skirt glued to my knees, I was pretty sure the dress didn't do wonders—whatever they were supposed to be. I thought of the other girls traveling in jeans or shorts or whatever was comfortable. But it was a nice dress, and I'd better be careful not to rip it.

Aided by my shifting and pulling, the elastic top of my pantyhose had worked its way down and was eating into the soft flesh above my hips. Mother thought pantyhose were absurd. She thought I should wear something called a garter belt. "Why should you throw out two stockings when there's a run in just one? Waste not, want not."

As we bumped along, a soothing voice on the loudspeaker began to give us disaster information, and when I had my dress straightened and looked up, there was the stewardess Mother had ratted to, standing in the front of the cabin with a yellow oxygen mask over her mouth. All I could see were her eyes looking straight at me. That special eye. I hunched my shoulders and collapsed inward like a turtle.

There was an awesome roar, speed, my back pressed into the seat, and we were in the air. I was flying! The patchwork ground tilted up at us, then we straightened and settled into a steady hum.

But I was wired. It was going to be a long flight. And there were things to worry about.

What if my trunk hadn't arrived at camp? I'd packed it so carefully with all the required items from the camper's list and most of the optional—even swim fins and goggles which I'd probably never use. But the trunk went off a week ago, and if it wasn't at Camp Sunny Days when I got there, what would I wear? I could imagine myself rigid on a sailboat holding down the billowing skirt of my diagonally striped traveling dress and trying to keep my new flats out of the cockpit water. That's what I'd look like if my trunk got lost—like Mother in her hat and gloves at the airport surrounded by moms in sundresses and running shorts.

Another worry: Would I be the only girl who

hadn't brought riding jodhpurs? I'd wanted them so badly, picturing myself swaggering around in those balloony pants like the self-confident girls in the Camp Sunny Days movie. But jodhpurs, it seemed, came only in very small sizes. In the three stores Mother and I tried, there were none I could even zip.

And what if they put me in the lowest swimming group, or what if someone tried to make me dive from the high board? And who was this person who was going to be my counselor, someone named Debbie Sue? Would a counselor be more like a mother or a stewardess?

A candy bar, that's what I needed. I looked in my purse. I pawed through my canvas gym bag. Where was my candy? I poked my hand again into the zipped side pocket. Nothing.

I'd forgotten a secret candy supply. And candy was my protection against stewardesses. Candy made trunks arrive on time. It was my consolation for not finding jodhpurs that fit. It made me feel—at least while I sucked and chewed and swallowed—the way I imagined other girls always felt. At ease. Confident. I needed that secret helper.

The "free to move about the cabin" announcement had been made, and suddenly there was Louise in the aisle. She reached over the top of my seatmate's head and tapped me on the shoulder. "Come on, sit with us for a while. We're in the way back, with three seats and two people."

"But I can't. This is my seat assignment. You're not supposed to change seats."

"Everyone does it. Don't be stupid."

I may have been stupid not to bring my candy, but there was no way anyone was going to find me stupid at Camp Sunny Days. If that's what everyone did, I'd do it. I scanned the aisle for that stewardess. Empty. This was my first chance to get close to Louise, and I'd grab it. I walked up the aisle, gripping onto the backs of seats in case the plane dropped, into the stale air of the smoking section in the rear.

"Hi Betsy-babes," Louise said in a new, silky voice, low and slippery. "Welcome."

Welcome. The same word she'd used when, as president of the block club, she finally decided I could take the test. Welcome.

The way Louise smiled at me now seemed just like her voice—friendly, but somehow oily. "This is Maxine," she said, wagging her thumb at a girl sitting by the window. "We thought you'd like some company." She patted the seat in the middle.

I hesitated. Lately Louise hadn't been worrying at all about whether I wanted company; in fact, she'd called me just last week to threaten me. The flash memory made my insides tighten.

"Betsy-babes? Listen. I'm going to make this clear. *Real* clear," she'd said menacingly. "I've been going to Sunny Days for three years now and I've got my own group of friends there, see?"

She'd paused to let me see it: Louise with her curly, shingled haircut and pouty mouth, her body petite but powerful enough to be captain of the field hockey team, moving always in her clique of popular friends.

"And I have no intention of being slowed down by some younger kid hanging on me. Don't forget it was your mom and my mom that cooked this up. Just because we live on the same block doesn't mean I have to take care of you."

"I don't need anyone to take care of me, Louise," I'd yelled into the phone.

"Just consider this a warning, Betsy-babes." The phone had clicked off gently.

As Louise swung her legs into the aisle, I climbed into the middle seat.

"You've known her a long time?" Maxine asked Louise, leaning over me, her blonde hair a curtain in front of my face.

"Yup, Betsy-babes has lived on my block since she was born. I've known her since she was a wee, piddling thing, right?" She looked at me for confirmation, as though this was the most natural question in the world. "I mean we're all real fond of this tyke. Just to prove it, we initiated her into our block club, didn't we Betsy-babes?"

"Oh Louise, quit living in the past. That was years ago; I can hardly remember it." But of course I did, every second. From the moment Louise had tightened the blindfold and the world turned mottled black, I'd been afraid.

"Well, actually we had to," Louise continued. "I mean she was trying to peep in the basement window all the time—so we gave in and initiated her."

I remembered hearing the thick wood door creak behind me, then Louise told me to strip and the other girls laughed. I refused. "This is your only, and I mean only chance to join this club," someone threatened.

I heard them snicker as I pulled off my shirt. Someone poked a finger firmly in my belly as though testing a cake for spring-back quality. I was trembling and prayed the girls thought it was cold, not fear.

"You should have seen her shake when we told her to walk over a floor of real, live worms," Louise howled, head thrown back.

I remembered that first step forward, and the slick squiggles I felt sliding through my toes. Then they ordered me down on hands and knees to wallow in them. My knees would barely unlock, but I did it. I knelt, mashing wormy things under my weight. I didn't scream or whimper.

"What was the next test?" Maxine gasped, barely recovered from her laughing fit. "The bowl of slimy eyeballs?"

"Oh come on, I knew those were grapes. Everyone knows that trick," I lied. My fingers had stiffened at the mere touch of those round, wet, jelly-firm things, while words from my science book—*iris, cornea, pupil, retina*—slithered through my head.

"So then what happened? That wasn't all, was it?"

"We took her outside."

"Still naked?"

"As a jay bird. Told her there were boys watching." Louise tossed her curls jauntily as though there were boys watching her this very moment, leering in the airplane window.

I couldn't stand listening to this. If only there were some way to plug invisible cotton in my ears or make my mind go as blank as eyes under a blindfold.

"So I grabbed her arm and said 'Up the stairs.

Turn. Okay, four steps straight ahead. Now stop.' "

"Where am I? What's going on?" I remembered I
said that word for word.

"You're out on my balcony," Louise said. "We've
made a gangplank for you. But don't worry, Betsy-
babes, it's only one story to the ground, just the height
of the apple tree. Now do it or I'll push you. Jump."

Once when I was very small I'd stood on a high
dive, panicked at the end of the board. "Jump,
Sweetie, jump!" Mother called from the side of the
pool. "There's nothing to it, I promise you. Go ahead
and jump, everyone's watching!" I'd been frozen with
fear, looking at the electric blue of the water and the
white tiles shimmering below its surface. I couldn't
move. "Really, Precious. It's not such a big thing. Just
hold your nose and jump." Mother sounded irritated.
I backed down the ladder slowly, in disgrace, gripping
the railing and curling my toes around each rung.

"Go on Betsy-babes. It's not such a big deal to jump
one story. That's only about twenty feet."

I took a huge breath on the gangplank and held it
the way I imagined you would if you jumped from
the high dive. For some reason it seemed easier to
have ground rather than water beneath me. In terror
I spread my arms, thinking that would help me soar.

A second later I was face down on the ground,
both ankles terribly painful. Blood oozed from my
thighs; gravel was embedded in my knees. The
ground had been only six inches from the gangplank,
and I'd hit hard.

"And the crazy thing is that the week after her
initiation the club disbanded," Louise told Maxine.

"It was one of those childish things we all outgrew, you know?"

I knew it took me months to get over being furious at them, Louise especially. I never got a chance to come to even one of their meetings. I never learned one single, dumb secret. Maybe I still wasn't through being mad at Louise, because a tingle started behind my eyes. My throat tightened.

"My goodness you did take it hard," Louise said, looking at me for the first time. "But we'll probably get something together when the summer is over—a sorority or something."

I didn't know whether to believe her or not. Anyway, I didn't know exactly what a sorority was. I thought it had to do with a coed, which is what Mother said Debbie Sue, my counselor-to-be, was.

"Hey Betsy-babes. Got something for you." Louise had her friendly smile back on. "Your ol' pal Louise has just what you need. You think she doesn't know after all these years? Guess again. She always does." She rooted in her purse. "Hang on, Betsy-babes. It's here somewhere."

Did I imagine it, or did she wink at Maxine?

A Heath bar. Oh yes, she did know, for Louise pulled out a Heath bar. Gratefully I unwrapped it. An expert, I nibbled the chocolate off a corner without nicking the hard, golden middle. Of course it scared me that Louise knew. On one hand I was glad, for here was candy—that glorious sweetness—when only a few minutes ago I'd been without hope. But I'd better watch out if Louise really understood how much I needed candy.

"Want another, Betsy-babes?"

Of course I did. Relief began to move through me. If Louise—who'd never given me a thing before—would hand out candy bars, then think what a place that camp must be. The girls were going to be wildly generous, just the kind I wanted for friends. And the proof was Louise digging through her purse again.

"Oh dear. All gone." Louise sounded as though she were talking to a baby who'd finished up her mashed bananas. "But that's all right, you don't need more candy now, do you?" She scratched in her purse, shaking it around. "Well my goodness, look what I found."

I stared. No, it wasn't a Heath bar she brought out; it wasn't a Snickers and it wasn't a Hershey. It was a pack of Marlboros. Louise shook out a cigarette.

Not for me, I thought, panicked, not for me. I was supposed to get the Heath bar. My blood slowed. There were no polite questions being asked: Have you ever smoked a cigarette? Would you like to try one? It was the club initiation again. I needed time.

"Are you sure there's no more candy?" My voice felt as though it was coming from a tiny opening in the back of my throat.

"Nope. Those kiddie days are over. Here we go Betsy-babes, welcome to the grown-up world. It's smoke time." And now Louise winked openly at Maxine.

A nervous balloon pumped up inside, pushing my stomach and shrinking my lungs. Oh my God, what if I were somehow caught breaking rules my first day as a Sunny Days camper? What about the stewardess lurking in the aisle? I'd planned to try it some time, but not here, not thirty thousand feet in the air. It wasn't that I thought smoking was so terrible, even though Mother and Daddy said it was disgusting.

Louise lit Maxine's cigarette, then her own. "Everyone, but everyone smokes at Camp Sunny Days," Maxine said, apparently talking to me for the first time. "Absolutely everyone."

"Where?" I squeaked out, stalling. Could I really be the only one in camp who didn't smoke? Would that be like being the last girl in seventh grade to get a bra?

"The Brown, silly."

Silly was better than stupid. I'd go no further. I wouldn't ask what the Brown was, though I guessed it was a secret clearing in the woods. A place for sororities.

Maxine jerked her jaw and exhaled a wavy doughnut.

I coughed.

"Well, look, Betsy-babes," Louise said, her voice matter-of-fact, "if you're too young just forget it. Maybe sometime when you grow up." She shook the Marlboro she'd aimed toward me back into its pack.

There was no way out. Either I was a nerd or I wasn't. I was pushed to the end of the gangplank; it was real, I could tell, for my toes felt the drop ahead. No way out at all. I saw a flash of metal from the lighter as I reached for the Marlboro.

Smoke chased through my blood stream, separated my head from my neck and sent it spinning, whirling.

I squeezed my eyes shut to slow the dizzies. Something sloshed inside my stomach and I stopped breathing. Finally I let out my breath and swallowed the sourness bubbling up my throat.

"Hey! Get a load of her!"

Their words came in slow circles, fading in and out.

"She loves it, don't you Betsy-babes?"

I felt terrible.

"Not bad. You really inhaled." Maxine sounded impressed.

Louise and Maxine mouthed big, wide, laughing smiles, round and dripping as a smoke ring. I tightened my upper lip, which I guessed was sweating, and hoped it passed for a smile too. When I looked at my hand balancing the cigarette I thought I might see someone elegant with tapered fingers tipped in red ovals; instead I saw my own stubby fingers and ragged nails.

Back in my own window seat I dozed away the rest of the trip with jerky, unpleasant mini-dreams. As the plane landed I sniffed my traveling dress for smoke smell. Cautiously I looked for the stewardess, but she was nowhere around. Some good she did. Some special eye.

3 ✳ Nine Iron Beds

I stood by the tree as I was told. The sign nailed to it said *New Girls* in red letters that dripped paint like tears. Ever since the rickety yellow school bus had shaken to a stop in front of the Camp Sunny Days lodge, the old girls had known just what to do. They'd been screaming, so I cleared my throat and yelled, "Wa-hoo!" The instant I heard my voice I knew it sounded nervous and forced, the kind of old-fashioned cheer Mother might give. The returning campers scrambled off, pushing over the knees of new girls, stepping on our feet. You certainly could tell the greeners. I stood slowly, plucked my dress off my sweaty thighs, and straggled out.

"New girls to the Meeting Tree," scratched a voice through a bull horn. "All new girls report to the Meeting Tree." So I stood at the base of this tall, skinny pine, with everyone yelling around me.

"Ruthann! Ruthann! Did you make cheerleader?"

"You bet! First squad!" A spunky girl with carrot curls vaulted into a split jump.

"Holy cow, what did you do to your hair?" screamed another camper. "You've had a perm!"

I touched my hair, but it was still straight. She wasn't talking to me.

Most new girls had been fetched by their counselors. Just a few of us were left by the Meeting Tree, trying not to look at each other. Suddenly I saw Louise starting up the hill, her back to me. Even though I'd vowed to stay as far away as possible, I couldn't resist using her as an excuse to leave the tree. I suppose I also wanted to show anyone looking that I wasn't such a tenderfoot—I knew an older camper. I dropped my suitcase, ran over, and tapped her shoulder.

As she spun toward me I saw the same welcome smile I'd seen a few hours ago.

"Hey, buzz off. Don't try to hang out with me all the time," she hissed through her smile.

I jerked around and went back to the tree. Louise could go to hell. Campers were swirling about, but I was alone at the tree looking for a counselor named Debbie Sue. I had no idea what she looked like. If *she* didn't know who *she* was looking for, we were sunk. I shivered self-consciously in the heat. And I was hungry. If only I had some Milk Duds this wait might be bearable.

"Cabin Five?" A counselor bounded up and looked sideways at my name tag. "Betsy?"

Debbie Sue burst in on my misery like a rainbow on a drizzling day. She wore a lavender T-shirt tucked into bright red shorts. Her blonde hair was almost white and shone like sunlight on satin. There were highlights of gold in her brown eyes, and her legs were amber below her shorts. Best of all, her smile beamed out for me alone.

"Hiya Bets!"

Debbie Sue had shortened my name, made it into a puffy sound like a chicken cluck. It sounded good; a completely new name for a new person. A Sunny Days camper.

"Here's the drill." As Debbie Sue threw a companionable arm around me, I could smell her clear lemon scent. "Everyone else is already in the cabin, but before I take you up there, you have to meet Miss Mack. That's the rule. She wants to be introduced personally to each new girl."

"Who's Miss Mack?"

"Where have you been, kiddo? I didn't think anyone could have heard of Camp Sunny Days without knowing who she is."

"Well I've never heard of her and I'm here," I snapped, and then felt embarrassed.

Debbie Sue laughed light and cascading, like a stream bubbling over smooth stones, trickling off into words. "You bet you're here—in fact very much here, I'd say. Grab your gym bag."

As we started down a narrow birch-flanked path, I realized Debbie Sue hadn't answered my question. "So who is she?" I asked again.

"Just the founder and guiding spirit of Camp Sunny Days, that's all. Thirty-seven years on the job and still going strong, I can promise you that. You'll see."

Debbie's voice dropped to a whisper. "Look, there she is."

Light filtered mistily through the pine trees as though they were hung with gauze. In a circular clearing with a pine-needle carpet sat an ancient woman, enthroned on a straight-backed chair. From the way she held herself, it seemed she should be wearing a velvet gown and sipping tea from a gilt-edged china cup. Instead she wore biker's shorts so tight they seemed to be squeezing out pale, veiny legs below her knees. Laced firmly over her ankles were black high-tops, the kind boys wear to play basketball.

"Missmack." I whispered her name quickly under my breath, and it sounded like a breeze whistling through the evergreens. "Missmack."

She was shuffling through a manila folder and didn't look up as Debbie Sue and I approached. When we were closer, I found myself staring into the caverns of a wrinkled turkey face. Skin flaps hung under the camp director's chin in long stringy folds. I found I wanted to touch the creases that cross-hatched her neck to see how deep they were.

Miss Mack's face jerked up. I think she knew she was being stared at; she looked full and hard at me, not smiling.

"What's your name, dear?" She had a high, thin voice which seemed not to come from her mouth but her nose. Her nostrils flared as she spoke.

"Betsy," I said softly. How I wished Mother was here to slip an arm around my waist.

"How do you do, Betty." Miss Mack inclined her

head slowly, the way a queen might recognize her subjects.

"No, my name's Betsy." Then in case she hadn't heard—because I saw no signs of enlightenment on Miss Mack's face—I repeated it louder, my lips tightly forming the sound: *"Betsy."* I could hear my voice ring out through the silent woods. Apprehensively I looked around at Debbie Sue. She winked.

"Of course. How rude of me to get your name wrong. Forgive me. We'll start over. How do you do, Betsy." Although Miss Mack's words sounded frosty, I thought I saw those puckered mouth-wrinkles begin to turn up like the sliver of a new moon. If only she'd smile, I thought, I'd have some proof we were really starting over.

"Bets is in Cabin Five with me, Miss Mack," Debbie Sue piped in. "I can tell already she's going to be a great Fiver."

"Most certainly she will be." Miss Mack smiled now that she was talking to Debbie Sue. But those wrinkles trembled as the smile disappeared; she shuffled papers again, then looked seriously up at me.

"Yes. Betsy Sherman, from St. Louis. Louise Paxton's mother recommended you, I see."

"Yes ma'am." I remembered how annoyed Mother had been when the form arrived asking for a reference. "Surely that camp knows I'm of good character," she'd huffed.

"Louise is a fine camper, one of our most attractive girls," Miss Mack said distractedly, still looking through the folder. She glanced back at me. "I must say, you don't look much like the picture you sent."

That's something to be thankful for, I thought. The Sunny Days application had asked for a recent snapshot. I couldn't find anything at home. "There must be one around someplace," Mother had said casually. But I stewed. I found myself in the family photo album as a cute, bald baby. I searched through stacks of white bordered glossies in the desk drawer and found myself at nine, then ten. After that no pictures had been taken. Why? I suspected but really didn't want to know.

The next week Mother and I went to Woolworths; inside a photo-cubicle I adjusted a lens, pulled a pleated curtain, and smiled each time the light flashed. A minute later the machine spit a strip of four head shots into Mother's hand. They were washed out, as though they'd been developed in Clorox. My jaw seemed swollen. I looked bug-eyed and desperate. "I look horrible, Mother," I'd said. "Pasty and shiny. Come on, let's ask for our money back."

Mother shrugged, then kissed the top of my head. "Oh goodness, Darling, they'll do. It's not worth the fuss."

Now if I could grab that nasty photograph off the application and rip it up I would. But Miss Mack seemed hardly the sort of person who'd let you grab anything. I stared down at my new flats, shiny as a photograph against the brown pine-needle ground.

Miss Mack cleared her throat, snorting out her nose. "I guess we've all had off days in front of the camera, haven't we?"

"You bet Miss Mack. You should see some of the

beauts that've been taken of me." Debbie Sue nodded gravely.

"Debbie Sue my dear, you could never be anything but lovely in a picture," Miss Mack said. I looked again at Debbie Sue. It was true, every photograph would capture her dazzle.

"Come here dear, let's shake hands and be friends. You're a lucky girl to be with our Debbie Sue. Now posture perfect, I expect you to have a fine summer."

What, I wondered, does she mean, "posture perfect"? Miss Mack's large hand, with bony knobs for knuckles, drifted toward me. Still a little nervous, I put my hand in it and found it surprisingly soft, like a well-used sponge.

When our hands came apart, something warm and a little gooey had been pressed into my palm. I didn't dare look. Perhaps a piece of Miss Mack's flesh, a wart maybe, had stuck to mine from nervousness. The idea made me feel feverish and my stomach sour.

"Debbie Sue, dear, take this young lady along to meet her cabinmates." Miss Mack had risen, back as straight as if she were a giant marionette being pulled from heaven. She continued to rise onto the toes of her black high-tops and bounced there, hands clasped primly in front of her.

"What an oddball," Debbie Sue chuckled when we were far enough away. "The last of a breed. Sometimes it's hard to believe there's such a character as Miss Mack—or a place like Sunny Days for that matter. But just go along with whatever she says, Bets, and you won't have any problems."

I let Debbie Sue move ahead of me, then carefully brought my fist up close to my eyes to peek at whatever horror had come off Miss Mack's hand. My fingers unwound slowly. And there it was. Square, chocolate, a little melted, but maybe even covering a caramel— candy! Amazing. Miss Mack had passed me a candy right in front of Debbie Sue. Nothing for her, only me. I'd been in this place less than an hour and already I had a secret. Candy! I molded it in my fingers. I'd never have guessed—Miss Mack, a candy person. Now we could really get along. Now I had an ally at this place.

I remembered the camp movie I'd seen last winter. Campers crouched around a bonfire, heads tilted, mouths open like little birds waiting for worms. They looked up at the counselor who passed out crisp graham crackers and chocolate bars. They made them into sandwiches stuffed with charred, dripping marshmallows.

"Yum-ee!" the girls in the audience had shrieked. "Fat boy's delights!"

And that was it, the moment I knew I could handle Camp Sunny Days.

I popped the candy into my mouth.

"Hey, what's going on back there. You daydreaming already Bets?"

"Bets. Bets." I tried the new name again, whispering through the caramel as I followed Debbie Sue to the main part of the camp.

The cabins were screen boxes on platforms held out from the hillside by stilts, with mossy, shingled roofs overhanging like square coolie hats. Steep wooden steps mounted to each cabin. Debbie Sue had turned off the dusty trail and stood on a step, her arms crossed in a waiting position.

"Come on kiddo, you're slow as can be. Hurry up," she called.

"You're not carrying this bag," I said in one breath. What had been a gym bag now felt like a huge crate of math books. Furthermore there was a stitch in my side and a rock in my shoe. "And what does *slow* mean, anyway? In the Olympics if you don't win a gold medal they call you *slow*."

"You've got a point there, Bets," Debbie Sue laughed. "You got me that time. Guess your brain's not so slow anyway. But come on, move it, lose it, or build a fence around it!"

At the door of Cabin Five I kept my fingers locked tightly on my bag, though my arm ached. I squinted, rubbed my eyes with my knuckles, and found the little colored dots dancing under my lids less confusing than the scene in front of me.

How would I ever find a place in this crowded cabin? It looked completely filled. I couldn't imagine space for me. At home my room was all my own. Here suitcases and girls and heaps of clothing were all jammed into one tiny cabin smaller than my St. Louis living room.

"Okay Bets, there you go, that bed in the corner. It's saved just for you." Nine iron beds with dark striped mattresses were evenly spaced around the room; without our sheets and wool blankets they looked bleak, the way I imagined they'd look in an orphanage. At home my bed had a pink dust ruffle around the box springs. Here the flat pillow smelled mildewed, as though it had been stored in a raccoon's cave all winter. I tested the springs under the thin mattress with my fist before I tried my full body weight. It squeaked and bowed way down, but held solidly. One thing had gone right. I wasn't on the floor on top of a collapsed bed. No, two things had gone right. Next to the bed was Daddy's olive army trunk with all my clothes.

Debbie Sue clapped her hands. "Attention my little charges—or not so little as the case may be. We're all here now and it's time you got to know each other. First let me introduce myself." Debbie snapped her fingers and twirled in the center of the cabin, shimmering like a butterfly on a rose. "I'm Debbie Sue McCrackin. I'm a sophomore at Iowa State, a tried and true Kappa Kappa Gamma, the best sorority on campus, and I'm the only bona fide Scottish-ancestry majorette for the Iowa High Flingers!" I didn't know what those titles meant, but they seemed to delight Debbie Sue, and that was enough for me.

"Now let's see about you guys. In the bed by the door is Cammy Lyons. Take a bow, Cammy."

A girl across the room stood, put her palms together and bowed from the waist.

"And in the next bed is Glenda Herman, who's new this year. Let's see, humm, from now on I'll call you Herm-the-Worm!"

The girl with hair plastered against her head was skinny, but she didn't look much like a worm to me. I had no time to wonder how she liked her new nickname, because Debbie Sue was on to the next.

"Here we have—" Debbie Sue flourished an imaginary drum—"Miss Dawn Marks. And in the next bed is my old pal Julia, returning for her fourth Sunny Days Summer. And next to her, with the most glorious head of hair I've ever seen, is Wanda Suzicki."

I had to agree. This girl's hair wasn't what you'd call chic, but it was orange-pink and thick and frothed around her shoulders like a strawberry milk shake.

"And in that bed is Dede from Des Moines," continued Debbie Sue, pointing a manicured finger at the corner opposite me, "and next to her is Anna Banana." Anna was indeed long and a little thick in the middle. Debbie Sue had an eye for nicknames, I could see that.

"In the right-hand corner is our other new girl—Betsy Sherman—otherwise known as Bets."

I dreaded having all those eyes turn toward me, but I held up my hand and gave a little cakewalk wave I'd learned from Mother.

"And last but not least, here is the unforgettable Jolee Benson."

Debbie Sue twirled around once more. "There," she continued in her chirpy voice. "I want you all to be good friends and think of yourselves as sisters the way we do in the Kappa Kappa Gamma house."

Friends. Sisters. I could only remember somebody-the-Worm and Anna Banana, because their names told what Debbie Sue thought they looked like. And I knew no one cared about real names at this point. All they cared about was looks. The question was this: How pretty were these girls, or to put it more bluntly—how much prettier than I was?

To start with, which of the group had naturally curly hair? For someone with thin, straight hair like mine this was very important.

Then who had big boobs? "You're going to be a late bloomer, Darling," Mother had warned. "You really don't need a bra yet."

I looked around the room to see if anyone still wore braces. Mine had gone on when I was ten, but at least they weren't those huge metal caps that made your mouth into a zipper.

What about glasses? That was one I had escaped altogether.

And how did complexions check out? I had zits, but compared to some girls I didn't feel I had much of a problem.

I knew for a fact everyone was checking, measuring as they put away their city clothes. I breathed shallowly as I strained to hold in my stomach. If I were to let my muscles go, I knew my belly would fluff out like a plumped pillow. That would betray one of my worst points from the beginning.

Turning my back to the cabin to change clothes, I tugged off my dress, quickly put on the blue shirt and shorts uniform, tucked in my shirt—then changed my mind. It looked better out. At least it covered my stomach so I could breathe normally.

Everyone else had changed into shorts. It felt satisfying and reassuring, all that sameness. One good thing about uniforms was that no one judged you by clothes.

"Let's go, let's go," Debbie Sue singsonged as she scooted around the cabin collecting us. "It's supper time, kiddies. Let's chow down. First cabin to the lodge gets the best table."

Supper. I was the first camper out of the cabin. Nothing had passed my lips but that teasing piece of candy since lunch on the airplane. I was starved.

The lodge looked as though it had been built from giant Lincoln Logs. Campers pushed at the door, then burst into the big mess hall end to end with picnic tables. For all the confusion and strangeness, the room was familiar because of the cooking smells. The very same fog that hung above the counter of the White Castle, where I had my daily after-school burger, now climbed into the rafters of the lodge.

A hundred and fifty girls clambered onto benches. Their roar swelled louder and louder, like the junior high band tuning up. Suddenly, complete quiet cut the room.

Miss Mack had risen. Her chair scrape chopped off talk and laughter. Campers and counselors swiveled to face her. Her white crowned head bobbed up and down, so I knew those high-tops were doing the basketball bounce again. Without letting her shoulders fall forward an inch, Miss Mack rested her forehead on clasped hands.

"Oh Great Spirit who makes all our days sunny, look down into this room upon your beautiful campers." Miss Mack's mournful voice wuthered through the mess hall like wind through the pines.

I kept my chin down, but opened my eyes to look at Miss Mack, whose bounce had almost become a hop. This was like no grace I'd ever heard.

"Take these little rosebuds, let their petals open,

open, open into the full-blown flower of woman-hood." Arched back, she flung her arms toward the rafters. The camp knew the cue and hummed "Amen," a low bass chord. "Now posture perfect, dears." Miss Mack sat.

The clatter resumed. Steamy platters of pink-tan hot dogs appeared. There were baskets of soft, long buns. I loaded up my plate.

I noticed I was sitting next to something-the-Worm. I tried to remember her real first name as I poured catsup and spooned crunchy relish on my hot dog. I gobbled potato salad. There was no time to talk even if I'd known what to say, for my cheeks were full and my jaws were working hard. I helped myself to a third hot dog. Then I realized how far I really was from home. No mother voice scolded me: "Darling really. Think before each bite. Do you absolutely need that? Don't you think you've had enough?"

I felt a heat coming from the place next to me, the feeling you're being watched. It was true, the Worm was staring at my plate. Empty. I looked over at hers. Full.

"What's wrong?" I asked. "Don't you like the supper?"

"My mom won't let me eat hot dogs. They're loaded with nitrites." The Worm sounded miserable.

I nodded sympathetically. Mother was always talking nitrates and nitrites too, another in the list of hazards of the twentieth century. "Well, what about the potato salad? You could eat that couldn't you?"

"I'm sure it's made with imitation mayonnaise. I can smell the chemicals from here. My mom says,

'Never put anything processed in your mouth until you've read the label.' But I'm hungry." Worm looked as though her long neck could hardly hold her head up, her thin hand barely hold the fork.

"Come on now," I said, giving her a light poke in the ribs with my elbow. "Lighten up. Your mom isn't here, she can't see what you're eating. Maybe it is made with chemicals, but I promise the potatoes are real, and the whole thing tastes just great."

"I could never eat the hot dog. My mom's been a vegetarian since before I was born."

"So don't eat it. Tell you what, I'll help you out and eat half, just so your plate looks normal. You do the potato salad."

I watched the Worm take a small bite, opening her mouth just enough to let the fork in. Another bite, and she looked over at me and smiled. I smiled back as I ate her hot dog. All of it.

Thick china dishes were unloaded from trays and passed down the table. Butterscotch pudding! I sniffed with delight as I passed along dish after dish, checking out the size of each Cool Whip dollop. The Worm looked alarmed.

"Try it," I whispered. "Don't forget she's not here to check on you."

I licked my spoon, savoring even the metal that would hold the pudding. I licked it again when I'd scraped up every creamy speck. I leaned over to the Worm. "What are the chances of getting seconds around here?"

4 ✸ *Taking Stock*

Several days passed before I had time to think: Until then I was just too busy doing. Finally one night at twilight—that magic hour when the world sinks down—I managed to get alone. I sat with my back against an overturned canoe that divided me from a waterfront volleyball game and stared out into Lake Sunset.

Camp Sunny Days was mighty organized, which wasn't something I'd expected. Following rules and regulations had never been my strong point. Everything had to be in groups. Everything had to be on time. Counselors dismissed us from one activity and expected us instantly at another—a sense of timing I expected only in school or prison. Miss Mack put it in her strange words one night at the council fire. "Punctuality is paramount in an orderly society, girls. Keep no one waiting."

So we rushed from archery, canoeing, and tennis, to sailing, crafts, and riding. I liked most of those things, but I didn't like being bossed around. I kept telling myself I came here because my summers had been full of nothing to do. What position was I in to complain?

Also, there was no privacy at Sunny Days. Even now, alone for the first time, I felt guilty. I knew I should be practicing choral speaking, or at least playing in the volleyball game.

Maybe, I thought, if I'd gone to a camp that didn't have such an upbeat name like Sunny Days I'd like it more. Especially on rainy days. Mother had gone to Camp WaBaNoKee, a proud Indian name. "The best summers of my life were spent there," she said. Everyone loved Mother, she had tons of friends. She still does.

Most of the campers had been coming to Sunny Days for years. They were chummy with each other and already I could see the outlines of cliques. Worm was my friend, but she was different. Making friends with her had been almost like a trick; all I had to do was teach her to eat potato salad. I was glad that we were close, but I wanted more.

Then I remembered our first swimming lesson.

Freezing wind scrubbed my face. I scoured my shoulders for warmth, but all I succeeded in doing was polishing up gooseflesh. On shore I could see Debbie Sue waiting, hands on hips, her legs making a triangle with the beach. She fingered a whistle ready for a blast. As she sucked in air, her black tank suit rippled with her oiled body like seal skin in the sun. She made a trumpet of her hands.

"Swimmers ready!"

I stood shivering in Lake Sunset, the murkiest lake I'd ever seen. Weeds whipped my ankles and waves threatened my warmest places. There was only one way to do it. I hurtled forward in a belly flop. My arms became pinwheels and I kicked like crazy.

A whistle blast. I could hardly hear through the bathing cap they made us wear "to prevent ear infections."

"Float three minutes," Debbie Sue yelled.

I was good at that. I popped to the surface like a bobber on a fishing line.

"Backstroke, girls," came Debbie Sue's faint voice.

This gave me a chance to look around as I swam. In the distance I saw the Camp Sunny Days patrol boat, piloted by Dusty, Miss Mack's nephew and Camp Sunny Days' only man. I heard he spent every summer here opening and closing camp with Miss Mack. On the waterfront he supervised a work crew that pulled out the slimy weeds which threatened to overrun Lake Sunset. Swimming on my back I could see his head now, with short, fuzzed hair that made him look like an orange tennis ball. Most of the campers were supposed to be in love with him, but I didn't find him at all good looking. His chin and cheeks looked rough as a cheese grater. Also, Dusty had a glass eye. It never blinked.

Three whistle blasts. "Buddy check," Debbie yelled.

I swam as far as I could to shore, high over the mud, skimming the grasping weeds until I grounded on the sand. Struggling to my feet, I looked around for my buddy.

I didn't know her name, but I could recognize

her—a tall and slender girl who was beautiful even in the bathing cap that made us look bald. I figured she was probably just as snooty as she was pretty.

What a nuisance this all seemed, being hauled out just when we were used to the water. Of course we were all safe—wasn't that why Dusty sat all morning sunning himself in the patrol boat? Now they wanted us to hold hands and raise them high for the count, as though we'd just finished a boxing match.

Dusty continued to recline with his shirt off in the beached patrol boat. "Okay. I want you to gather round me," he yelled. One eye stared straight ahead while the other danced in different directions. "I'm head of the disaster squad, you understand?"

Campers nodded, shivering.

"Okay. I don't want you never, never to think of leaving this swimming area without your buddy, understand? Your buddy is the best friend you got on this waterfront, understand? Don't you never sneak off without her."

I glanced over at my beautiful, aloof buddy, and imagined her alone on the beach desperately looking for me. She'd be sobbing, pacing the sand. Dusty's patrol boat would circle the swimming area; I could almost hear the clank of chains and grappling hooks as they were lowered to scrape the lake's weedy bottom for my corpse. Debbie Sue would be frantic. Meanwhile, I'd be lying on my bed, wrapped in my warmest blanket, reading a soap opera magazine and munching potato chips.

No. I faced the wind and shimmied hard against the cold. Being tough is part of being a Sunny Days camper, I told myself—as though I were Miss Mack.

"Today I'm going to demonstrate one of the disaster techniques, you understand?" Dusty loped toward us on the beach, glass eye fixed while the other roamed over our shivering group. "Okay. Now I'm going to pick one girl for my demonstration." He bore down on us. His eye flicked over me and landed on my buddy. "This one," he said, grabbing her arm, leading her red-faced into the waist-deep water. Everyone giggled nervously. "Float," he ordered.

"Notice he always picks a beauty," Debbie Sue said to the group in a low voice. "Wait until tomorrow, you jealous damsels—he's going to demonstrate mouth-to-mouth resuscitation."

"Okay. This is the fireman's carry, understand?" Dusty waded to shore swaggering under the weight of my buddy flung across his back like a blue ribbon sack of wheat. He looked around triumphantly, then let my buddy drop. She slid down the back of his legs and hit the sand.

"How did you like your ride with Mr. Studly? Some macho-man, huh?" I whispered when my buddy picked herself up. I expected shiny eyes and sighs.

"Disgusting," my buddy hissed. "That guy's weird."

"What else is new." But I was glad for what she'd said. "If we're going to be buddies all summer I guess I'd better know your name," I said casually.

She gave me a neutral look, neither friendly nor unfriendly. She was quiet a moment too, as though she was trying to figure me out. Just when I thought she might walk away without another word, she put out her hand.

"Lolly Sharp."

That was all, just Lolly Sharp. . . .

I wiggled against the overturned canoe to scratch my back, and as I did, a little burp came up. It brought my thoughts back to food.

I looked forward to supper more than any other time. Worm and I sat together at every meal, and we always had a lot to talk about. That night after the swimming I saw Lolly too—it was impossible to miss her since she was the center of a group of popular, older campers. We crowded up for supper outside the lodge door, and Lolly was at the front of the pack. I admired her for that. When she caught my eye she gave me the thumbs-up sign.

"Hungry! Hungry! Hungry!" we all screamed at the locked door.

"Where's your manners?" yelled the cook. "No food for anyone who pushes." She unlatched the door in her own good time. Campers poured in like unplugged catsup, a glug as Lolly and her friends went in first, followed by an out-of-control flow.

"You sure do love to eat," Worm said as I filled up my plate.

"It's a lot better here than at home. Daddy always carves, then serves these tiny portions. And the plates have to be warmed just so, or he sends them back to the oven."

"There's nothing to carve at our house. I don't think I'd even know how to chew meat."

"You like all those vegetables?" I asked.

"Most of them."

"Even the stuff like creamed cauliflower?"

"Yuck."

"Yuck is right. And Mother always makes me eat it. 'You must try a little of everything, Darling.' " It was my best imitation.

Worm laughed. That's one thing I really liked about her—she appreciated my acting ability.

"Then I have to wait to begin eating until we're all three served and Mother has lifted her fork."

"Don't tell a soul, but we use chopsticks."

"Even with fried eggs?"

"We don't eat eggs. Mom would die if she knew what I eat here. I couldn't figure out why she let me come to Sunny Days, except that I had to go somewhere this summer so she could go do her own thing."

"What's that?"

"A two week meditation in a Buddhist monastery. Then Tai Chi camp."

"Oh." I was quiet trying to imagine what those things were. "Well, it's lucky she let you come. Did she have any idea what they serve here?"

"Not really, but she always says, 'A vegetable is never very far away.' And she said she trusted me to make responsible judgments about my food."

"You're doing just fine," I said, patting her back.

And then there was dessert. Lemon pie with glossy meringue like sweet, chewy clouds. The day before it had been strawberry ice cream and the comfort of Oreo cookies. And before that devil's food cake, icing studded with dark, shaved chocolate. It seemed like heaven after my St. Louis life where, on the rare occasion that we had dessert, it was a melon slice decorated with a mint leaf.

While I ran my empty fork between my lips searching for lingering crumbs, the after-supper camp songs began. Miss Mack bounced to standing position, tapping on her glass with a knife.

"Sweet girls, attention! Let me give you the note." She warbled one note that knocked against two others in her throat.

As my shoulders jerked back and chin clamped down, my splendidly full stomach reached for my spine.

"Posture perfect, posture perfect,
Do not slump! Do not slump!
Straighter you must sit up
Straighter you must sit up
Hide that hump.
Hide that hump."

We stretched our necks and arched our backs. Only our jaws moved as we sang; there was no swaying, no nodding, no clapping. Miss Mack conducted with her knife, slicing the air with the blade. I kept my head straight forward, but cut my eyes to the side. Was everyone else posture perfect?

Yes, they were. Absolutely perfect. Even Worm. And especially Lolly.

Muscles twitched between my shoulders. I wasn't meant to sit this way, it was unnatural. What I needed was a nice, cushiony armchair.

Very slowly, as though a tiny pin had pricked my

chest, I began to exhale the deep breath that held me up. I slouched. I could see Louise and her friends sitting straight as concrete walls. I slouched some more, until I was back to normal. No one seemed to notice. . . .

On the beach I found I was holding my breath and letting it out slowly, as I would if it really had been posture-perfect time, instead of a few minutes alone. In the fading twilight Lake Sunset looked black and oily, as though mud had boiled up from the lake bed to grease the top. The volleyball streamed over the net like a meteor, and campers jumped for it in the dark. Little shouts and laughter pierced the evening. St. Louis seemed thousands, not just hundreds of miles away.

At this very moment Mother must be dressing for a restaurant, or perhaps a party. I could see her at her vanity table, in front of her art deco mirror. She'd tighten her lips, then outline them in the faintest peach color with a tiny brush. She touched loose powder to her nose. I was the one who always fastened the clasp of Mother's pearls—who was doing that tonight? She'd ask me to check her out: Was the ruffled petticoat peeping perfectly below her prairie skirt? Did I like her new earrings? Daddy would go out to start the car.

All my life I'd been with my parents. I'd always had the same friends. When I went to seventh grade I changed schools, but so did my classmates. They were the same ones I'd had since kindergarten.

Here at Sunny Days there were so many unknown

girls. I was watching. I eased behind little groups. When we changed activities I lingered behind couples, listening. I knew the signals. If a pair looked back, giggled and pulled themselves tighter, I didn't bother with them again. But if they spread out to make room for me, or if one dropped back to walk with me, I didn't let the chance slip by to make friends.

These campers came from all over—Keokuk, Twin Cities, Chicago. The only thing they knew about me was that Debbie Sue liked me, Lolly Sharp and I were swimming buddies, and Worm was my best friend. Louise was four cabins up the hill and so far she'd ignored me. It seemed this was the first time I could be liked for who I really was, not for whoever I'd been the year before. I had a feeling, something like a giggle you can't let out, that there was something very special about me no one had yet discovered.

Of course there was the problem of good looks, but that would pass. It couldn't be the most important thing forever.

A memory popped up, one I didn't especially want right now. Two years ago a strong and wiry boy in my class challenged me to a wrestling match.

"Come on Betsy, you're broad as a sow. You ought to be able to beat me."

I desperately wanted to do that. I wanted to prove that being big was worth something. I wanted to cream him, so he'd understand his insults were nothing. It was spring, and the match was held during recess in a back soccer practice field. The entire class came. Secretly I felt I was representing all the girls.

"I wouldn't go through with this if I were you,"

my friend Isabel warned. "That guy knows what he's doing."

"You just watch," I said in my toughest voice. My insides were shaking.

That skinny boy pinned me in seconds, wrenching my arm on the way down, then kneeling painfully on my stomach. He flattened my cheek into the dirt with his hand.

I never cried, though I hurt all over. Kids laughed, yet I felt they couldn't help but be proud of me for daring. I cleaned myself with paper towels in the girls' room and never told my parents. Sometimes when I tear a wing off a piece of chicken I think of that boy.

5 ✸ No Way Out

"Come on."

"Who me?"

"Come on, shake a leg. Get up."

I was gorged. I sat swollen in the sun, my face turned up, eyes shut. The elastic back of my Sunday shorts was stretched tight, biting into my skin. My shirt buttons strained in their holes. I didn't care. I'd waddled from the lodge and collapsed on a grass patch that looked as welcome as land to a shipwreck survivor. I leaned back on my elbows to give my lungs room for small gulps of air. Sunday dinner was now in my belly.

At noon all the Sunny Days campers had dressed in our special uniforms—creased white shorts, crisp white shirts, new white running shoes. We looked pretty gorgeous, I must say. There was something about all that blinding white that made us seem pure and above our weekday selves. Like goddesses we drifted down to the lodge for Sunday dinner. When I saw the picnic tables transformed by sheets into an elegant dining hall, I knew a feast was coming.

Fried chicken with puffed and golden crunchy coating was piled high on platters. The very smell of it made me think of my birthday, when I could ask Mother to cook whatever I wanted.

"It's my top favorite dinner in the world," I said to Worm as we climbed over the benches and took our places.

Worm, however, looked waxen. "I've never eaten fried chicken. I pretended to at a friend's house once, but really I cut it up and fed it to the dog under the table."

I stared at her in disbelief. Life without hot dogs was one thing, and I could see how a vegetarian might find it hard to attack a juicy slice of roast beef. But fried chicken! "You mean you've never even been to a Kentucky Colonel drive-in?" I stammered.

"Mom would die. She thinks that guy's the devil himself. She'd rather be fried in a vat of oil—as long as it's unsaturated—then eat the flesh of a bird."

"Worm. Listen. You're among friends now. Try one little piece. Give it a nibble. It's not going to hurt you, I promise."

"You really think it would be okay?" Her forehead was wrinkled up like a pug dog's, and her eyes begged for permission.

"Of course. Look around you, what's everyone else eating? Does this look like a group at death's door? Worm, I'm telling you, this is the summer to loosen up. Here, try a thigh." I put one gently on her plate.

" 'The closer the bone, the sweeter the meat,' " I quoted, and sank my teeth into a drumstick.

I loaded slices of jellied cranberry sauce on my plate. In a mountain of mashed potatoes I made a deep crater lake, filling it with thick, dark gravy.

"I can't believe how good this is," Worm said, pecking at the crisp chicken.

"Can you send the corn around again?" I rolled the ears in melted butter, lifted them dripping, and put two more on my plate.

"Corn is one of the great grain staples of the world," Worm added solemnly between chicken bites.

At last came the glory of glories—ice cream sundaes with steamy fudge sauce and a mound of whipped cream swirled on top. It seemed like only seconds before I'd finished every little bit—then found myself looking with envy at Worm's dish. It was incredible. She had barely begun her sundae; in fact, she was playing with it, spooning up only the melted ice cream at the edges. I slid closer. Though completely full, I'd gladly stuff in another dessert if I got the chance.

"Does your mom let you eat ice cream at home?" I said as an opener.

Worm pulled her hand around her sundae, safe-guarding it. "We don't buy it, but sometimes my mom makes it. Of course she uses honey instead of refined sugar. Tastes pretty good, too." Worm's spoon traveled slowly to her mouth. "And so does this."

It seemed clear she was going to eat her own dessert, so I changed the subject. I'd been strangely embarrassed to ask about this rumor I'd heard, but Worm and I were good friends now. She'd understand. I rubbed my palms together. "I hear good ol' Sunny Days lets us have one candy bar a week, and that happens to be on Sundays. Today is Sunday."

Nothing. No reaction from Worm.

"Well? When's it coming, do you know?"

Worm looked over at me with a funny, wobbly grin. "Goodness Bets, I can't believe how much you eat. How could that stomach of yours hold anything else?"

I felt myself grow hot. I looked down at my empty dish so she wouldn't see my face. "Congratulations, Worm. You've managed to sound exactly like my mother on one of her bad days."

"Sorry. That was lousy. Erase the last statement. And to answer your question: I think they give out candy bars tonight, after Sunday supper."

Like a cash register, the word *candy bar* rang up a Hershey in my mind. Somehow, full as I was, I left the lodge with that image in front of me and still had it as I stretched out on the grass, dreaming and digesting. With my eyes closed, I could actually see the dark brown wrapper with silvery letters. I remembered how the waxy liner slid out, ends folded cleanly under. I saw the Hershey scored in ten squares and imagined breaking one off, pushing it to the roof of my mouth to ooze down my throat. I had been five whole days without candy. . . .

"Listen kid, I said get up," a voice barked.

Could someone really be talking to me? I wondered. My eyes opened to a girl standing above me, arms sternly crossed. I didn't know her, but she was clearly addressing me.

"This is the last time I'm telling you to come on. Get on your feet. It's time for weigh-in."

Way-in, far-out, I didn't care which. I only wanted to sit in the sun. But it seemed I was trapped—this girl was determined to get me up. Reluctantly I pushed to a sit, went forward on my knees, and stood. She turned and took off, running to catch up with some girls walking down the trail toward the infirmary. I followed. Ahead I saw other groups of campers, so I began to get the idea: This was some sort of event for everybody. Something mandatory. Judging by the direction we were taking, it must be at the infirmary. I plodded on.

The trail ended at a clearing, where campers sat crosslegged on the ground in front of a small, brown, shingled house. Their backs were to me, and I noticed that while an occasional one slumped, most were posture perfect.

Two steps up on the wide porch that surrounded the infirmary waited Miss Mack, clipboard in hand, and a stack of manila folders on the table next to her. The camp nurse was there too, with a white winged cap pinned into her curls.

Without understanding exactly why, I felt as though a plug had been pulled in my feet and my blood had drained out. My heart banged uselessly in my chest.

From the sickroom, with its shuttered windows and jars of thermometers in alcohol, an ancient white platform scale had been rolled out on creaking casters.

It stood on the shaded porch—a gallows with an arm of numbers. Clanky gray weights dangled from hooks, and a menacing sliding pole waited to measure heights. Miss Mack and the nurse guarded it from both sides.

I stared at the thing as I sat down behind the other campers. Now I understood. There must be some way out of this weigh-in. At home I'd sometimes check my weight on Mother's little heart-shaped bathroom scale, looking quickly at the dial to see which big number it was near. That was close enough. I'd never wanted to know my exact weight.

"Girls." Miss Mack knocked a pencil against the porch railing for attention. "Girls girls girls. Let's have enough quiet please so we can hear our names. When I call you, be prompt."

Prompt. Was I near enough to the edge of the woods to promptly inch over, ease into the thicket, and wiggle off like a fat woodchuck?

"We've had a simply marvelous Sunday lunch, I'm sure we all agree. Now it's time to weigh in so we can show your parents how you're growing into splendid young women at Camp Sunny Days."

If I were to double over with a stomachache, or fall to the ground with a dreadful headache, would they each take me by an arm and help me through the door to the sickroom, bypassing the scale? I felt sure Miss Mack would do that—but the nurse, she was an unknown. It was her job, after all, to tell real sick from fake. I dared not try.

Campers were being called alphabetically. No one looked upset. There was no crying. I saw no one trembling. Nor had I heard anyone refuse to go. My fellow campers, in fact, looked happy and satisfied after their Sunday dinners. They talked softly, listening for their names. When they jumped up to answer the call, they gave each other pats on the rear like athletes on the bench allowed into a game.

"I'll save your place!"

"Hey Alice! Sit here when you're finished."

They ran to be weighed.

Although I wasn't close to the porch, above the gentle chatting of the girls I could hear every pound the nurse reported to Miss Mack. My shirt became wet under my arms.

"Catlin: 5 feet 3½ inches, 102 pounds." Catlin trotted back to her friends, smiling.

"Ferguson: 5 feet 1 inch, 98 pounds."

"Herman."

Herm-the-Worm's turn came and went quickly. She slipped up on the scale and weighed so little it hardly registered. As she came off the porch I could tell she was looking for me, but the wave I gave her was small and frightened. She didn't see it. If there was one thing I didn't need now, it was to be conspicuous.

"Paxton."

Louise. That was Louise. It made me nervous that Louise would hear what I weighed. I watched her thread her way through clusters of girls, hopping over knees and landing lightly in the smallest clearings. She bounced up the porch steps, then took the scale with a smile.

The nurse barked out names and numbers. Miss

Mack said nothing. She wrote in the folders without glancing up. Girls glided up the steps, stood still on the scale, and reached tall to have their heights measured.

"Posello: 4 feet 10 inches, 96 pounds."

"Rudd: 5 feet 5 inches, 110 pounds." Rudd didn't seem distressed. She saluted as she came off the porch.

They had finished the Rs. There was no escape.

"Saunders. Seligman. Shaw, Ellie."

They were close.

"Shaw, Patty."

They were almost there.

I was off the ground before my name was called. As I heard "Sherman," I was bounding up the porch stairs swift as anyone, praying my footsteps didn't sound too loud on the old wooden floor boards.

In front of the scale I had a last-minute idea. Why hadn't anyone else thought of this? I bent to untie my sneakers.

"Oh no you don't," said the nurse. "Shoes on."

I put one foot on the jiggly base and gently brought the other up slowly, lightly. Perhaps if I only touched the scale with one foot I'd weigh less.

"Turn," said the nurse, swinging my shoulders around.

My back was to the scale; my heels, rear end, and neck pressed against the pole. I looked out over the sprawl of campers and suddenly my friends were gone. I couldn't find Lolly or Worm or any of my cabinmates. There was just a nightmare audience of skeletons, all ghoulishly staring at me from bleached skulls.

"Posture perfect," said the nurse, poking at my shoulders.

Blinking and pulling in a deep breath, I aimed my head higher as a metal bar met it lightly on top.

"All right, now let's see what you weigh."

I released my breath and turned around to face the monster. This was it.

A fifty-pound weight was already in place. The nurse slid a twin down to join it, and as she did I was sure she glanced at my stomach in a disapproving way. On the top a ten pound weight clicked into place. If only she'd stop there. But I knew it, I knew it: Not enough. The nurse pushed down a second ten pounder and paused. A third. Pause. She looked at my stomach again and pushed on a fourth weight.

At last it was too much. The balance tilted, the gauge banged down like the gavel of a judge. The nurse added single weights, tapping them into place. The indicator steadied in the middle. The verdict was coming, and I could only hope for a last-second reprieve. Maybe a scramble in her brain would have her speak in Chinese.

"Sherman: 5 feet 5 inches, 144 pounds."

I took the two steps down in one leap.

"Wait a minute, dear." It was Miss Mack's voice coming over me like the swell of a wave. The camp director was speaking to me. All week I'd wanted to chat with Miss Mack, who'd made me feel so welcome and special with candy that first day. She'd been either not around or very busy. But she wasn't too

she was addressing. I turned to
~~gh~~, public voice held me stock

~~says~~ here in your record that your
~~s~~ you to lose weight at Camp Sunny

~~n't~~ know what . . ." I began.

~~ss~~ Mack interrupted. "Look. Just look right here
~~the~~ application letter." Firmly she passed me the
manila folder.

*"What single thing do you most want your daughter to
accomplish this summer at Camp Sunny Days?"* Miss Mack
read loudly.

The blank was filled in with big block letters in
Mother's handwriting.

LOSE WEIGHT.

What? I'd never heard words like that before from
Mother. She couldn't have written them. Mother
wanted me to dive from the high dive, she'd told me
so. She wanted me to climb those dizzying spiral
rungs and spring myself from the end of the board
to the water. That must be what she wanted.

"You see that? Your mother wants you to lose
weight. Now I think we've got our work cut out for
us." Miss Mack inclined her head sideways and looked
hard in my face. "Don't you?"

Cut out for us? Cut out her tongue, her mean,
hurtful tongue, that's what I'd cut out. I was paralyzed
at the foot of the steps thinking words I could not
say. This lady was supposed to be my friend. I looked
up at Miss Mack grown giant, with a booming voice.
It seemed all the campers on the lawn had become

quiet and were listening to us. A vibration b[
under my nose, turned to a throb, and spread to
temples. Tears were instant behind my eyes ar
slithered down my throat. My pounding head mad[
me nod to Miss Mack.

"We have many goals to reach this summer, and
this certainly is one of them."

"Yes ma'am," I managed to whisper.

Miss Mack's sharp beak face pressed forward, wat-
tles hanging, eyelids blinking rapidly. She waited. I
knew it was words she demanded, not dumb shrugs
and bows. If I couldn't make words, Miss Mack might
lecture me forever. Her turkey head wobbled to the
other side, waiting. The campers sat alert to hear
better.

"Use self control, dear." Miss Mack rubbed her
own flat stomach, bouncing on the toes of her high-
tops. "Eat sparingly. Take small bites and chew thor-
oughly. Exercise vigorously." She pumped imaginary
weights above her head.

I had to say something, start with one word, though
I wasn't sure what it would be. My throat fuzzed, my
mouth filled with cotton.

"Sure, Miss Mack."

I'd said it, I must have—I heard myself, I must be
the one. So I shifted my weight to one hip, hoping
that made me look casual. I had to show those girls
out there this whole business meant nothing to me.
At least there was a small victory—I wasn't going to
cry. More words came, louder and more confident.

"Don't worry."

My mother knew from hard experience what "don't

worry" meant, and all the campers knew what "don't worry" meant. But looking at Miss Mack's eyes, narrowed and unchanged, I was sure she did not. Don't worry meant: *Leave me alone.*

I saw the campers smiling, encouraging me with little giggles. They knew what was up. Like the great actress I wanted to become, I knew when I had my audience. I'd finish in style. So I started a chuckle that was low, a little intimate as though it was just between Miss Mack and myself, but then I let it burble on a second, for the campers, until it stopped on the edge of sarcasm. I shrugged.

"Really Miss Mack. No problem. I can handle it."

Immediately Miss Mack snapped back to her folders, as though I'd asked her advice and now didn't want to listen. She called the next name, dismissing me. As I took my seat on the grass again, I tried to hold my triumph in my eyes. The curtain had gone down. I could imagine the applause, the campers' secret cheers, and I held on to that, for if I let go there would be only one thing I could see: My own misery, misery, misery.

6 ✻ Eating Hollyclark Cake

Supper that night was horrible. I slunk in late planning to sit by myself, as far as possible from Miss Mack. If only her huge wrinkles would swallow her up, if only she could disappear into them like a dinosaur sinking into a bubbly tar pit. But life is never that fair, and there was Miss Mack in her usual place, bouncing around in her weird way, acting as though nothing had happened. And there was Worm, saving me a place and acting the same way.

"What's that junk?" I asked as the serving platter was passed around. It was filled with something messy, a gray-green yellow.

"Since when don't you recognize scrambled eggs? I beg your pardon—correction—it's boiled brains."

"Miss Mack's brains," I muttered, and passed them by.

The only other accompaniment to this sorry meal was carrot sticks, faded and rubbery, no doubt rejected by the horses. Dessert came—fruit cocktail with no grapes.

"You're going to eat that stuff?" I asked Worm, amazed. "It's been in a can so long you can taste the tin. Your mother would have a fit."

"Come off it Bets. It's one thing to feel sorry for yourself, but don't put your trip on me. Forget the whole business, is my advice. Miss Mack was butting in where she had no right to be. Everyone knows that."

At last Worm had mentioned it. No one else had said a word to me about my humiliation at the scale, but I was on guard, just waiting for the first snicker. And I was keeping special track of Louise—this was one thing I didn't want her telling the girls on the block at home. I could too easily imagine her making big barrel gestures with her arms, laughing and laughing.

I knew Worm was right—I should forget the whole business—but the director's nasty words would not go away. *I think we've got our work cut out for us.* When I was a little girl Mother brought me paper dolls to cut out; if they were too large I could cut them smaller. Of course they never were too large, they were perfect. The trouble was I couldn't cut myself smaller.

Now I was checking every camper's size, staring at them all, comparing myself part by part to each. There was only one conclusion: I was in deep trouble.

My hips weren't bony. My waist wasn't small. My stomach sloped out like a huge hamburger bun. My flesh folded in ripples when I bent to the side. Truth was, I hadn't seen my ribs since I was eight. As I poked through spongy tissue to feel them, I remembered the glistening fat layer on a roast beef, quivering as Daddy carved.

The inside of my knees looked like two hornets' nests attached to thick trees. They forced my ankles apart when I stood. There was no hollow place between my thighs, and they rubbed together—making that the embarrassing first place to wear out in my jeans. As for my rear end, it was frankly enormous. Until that day I'd rather liked it, for Daddy would pat it and call it my "tumba."

I saw there were a few other girls who were, well, heavy—but all of them seemed different. They were dignified. They seemed so confident, wearing their bulk like expensive down parkas—to keep them warm, to protect them. They couldn't feel the way I did. They were like the sleek, thin ones who never thought about their weight.

Now I could hardly remember what I'd been like before today, before I got the word my main problem was fat. I'd seen myself as just a kid with a hair problem and a few pimples waiting to be recognized as the terrific person I knew I was. Worm liked me, Lolly Sharp knew I existed, Debbie Sue and my cabinmates seemed to like me. True, Louise used to pinch my arms and say they felt like bread dough, but that was years ago.

The little arm-rub Worm gave me with her knuckles didn't feel at all like a pinch. "Hey wake up, Bets. We were having a conversation and you spaced out. This is your friend Glenda Herman talking."

"I know Worm. I just can't talk about it right now. I know you're trying to cheer me up and stuff, but I'd rather just drop the whole thing. Like you say, forget about it."

But it was Mother I couldn't forget. My very own mother, who'd always made me feel that my size was nothing to worry about. She'd called it "baby fat." And I'd assumed fat melted. One day, my rolls and thicknesses would dissolve—it would hardly involve me. I'd be reshaped graceful and willowy as Mother when the right time came.

I pictured her reading on the couch, her legs folded sideways, feet tucked under. Next to her on the coffee table was her lunch tray. Untouched. A silver fork gleamed on a folded napkin. Beside it was a lonely plate dotted in the middle with a spoonful of cottage cheese. Two peach slices decorated one side, and several grapes the other. That was all she ate between breakfast and dinner.

So, I realized, slenderness didn't just happen. There was a word for it, a word I'd heard a hundred times and never wanted to say. Diet. And there was a word for me, too. Fat. I was alone, plump, and flabby. My fat now seemed to hang loose around me, and I felt it bump and jiggle when I moved. Yes, I was in trouble. I'd heard it at last from Mother. LOSE WEIGHT.

But why hadn't Mother said this to me before? Why hadn't she put it in words? I remembered that once she'd said, "You're pleasantly plump, Sweetie, that's all." If we'd talked about it, nothing would have happened in the terrible way it did today. I wouldn't have been humiliated in public. And also, I could have asked the questions that churned inside me.

Mother, if I start dieting am I going to have to think about it for the rest of my life? Will I always eat dreadful cottage cheese lunches like yours?

Mother tell me, what's so good about thin anyway? Why does everyone praise it so? Why does everyone want it?

Mother—the truth. This is important. If I get thin will it make me happy? Will it solve all my problems? I remember reading that "a woman can never be too thin or too rich." Is that the secret of happiness? Does being thin somehow make you rich?

I ate the tasteless fruit cocktail, stirring the watery syrup and thinking it was the kind of thing Mother would like. Listlessly I watched as another tray slid down the table. Who'd want seconds of this terrible dessert? Then I focused. The tray was heaped with, piled and filled with—candy bars.

Almond Joy. Baby Ruth. Peppermint Patties. Milky Way. How I loved to say those names. At home Angelo the Candy Man parked his sky-blue van in front of the high school, lowered a flap, and displayed three tiers of candy bars. Even when there was a line behind me, Angelo would say, "Take your time kid. It's all you got." And I'd read all the candy names, whispering those sugary words aloud.

"One, only one," chanted the archery counselor as the tray was pushed slowly down the center of the table. "One, only one."

"Look what's coming," Worm said uneasily. I supposed her mom didn't allow her to have candy either, but I couldn't worry about that now.

At last, I thought, at long, long last.

Campers plowed into the heap, grabbing candy as the tray jerked nearer. It was mounded with goodies. There'd still be a good choice when it reached me.

With each inch the tray was pushed nearer me, I felt better. The closer it came, the more I remembered this was what I needed to cure my misery, to make me happy again.

"One, only one."

I spied the orange Clark Bar flagging me on to the finish like an Indy 500 winner. My arm shot across Worm and snatched the Clark Bar off the tray. It was mine.

"One, only one," the archery counselor warned.

Fast, I jammed the Clark Bar in my shorts pocket. I didn't know I was going to do this; I'd planned to do what the other campers did. They peeled back the wrappers and held their chocolate delicately. I wanted to be just like them. But look what I'd done instead, put the Clark Bar in my pocket. I watched the campers eat, earnestly chewing small bites, just like Miss Mack said. I wanted to eat that candy so badly two chomps of my jaws would gnaw it to a pulp.

"Hey Bets, I know you're finished, but do you think you could manage another?" It was Worm, passing a Tootsie Roll under the table into my hand. "I guess I got confused and picked the wrong kind. I really don't want this."

All right! That made two. "Hey Worm, old buddy old pal. Do you really know what you're doing? Or should we just enter an insanity plea and be done with it?"

"Don't give me a hard time. Take the thing—you like them and I don't. It's as simple as that."

"I accept, with gracious thanks." But I had to think fast. I suddenly knew why I had put my Clark Bar in my pocket. I didn't want the other campers to see me eating. I didn't need any more humiliation. Nothing must provoke their memory of the weigh-in. I gave Worm a wink. "I'm going to do this Tootsie in later, to make the pleasure last."

It was true. I wanted that sweetness to be mine alone, pure and private. I would take the Clark and Tootsie back to the cabin. Tonight, uninterrupted, without gawkers or comments, I'd have my feast.

After dusk I skulked off my white uniform. I stuffed myself into pajamas, careful not to expose my body to my cabinmates. Pickpocket quick I transferred the Clark Bar and Tootsie Roll from my shorts to my bathrobe. It was time to make my last trip to the Brown.

No, the Brown was not the wonderful campers' hideaway I'd imagined. It was the latrine. At home there was a gadget that turned our toilet bowl blue, and Daddy always insisted the bathroom be sprayed with lemon deodorizer after use. Here, we had twelve stalls perched over a long underground pit. The first few days it had smelled like raw chemicals. Now a stronger stench had taken over.

As I sat on the wooden throne, I was careful to hold my bathrobe pocket tightly. I pinched my nose and breathed directly down my throat with my mouth open. As always, I did my business as fast as possible and left quickly.

Then I went to the pump and brushed my teeth. As I spit foam from my green and white chlorophyll toothpaste into the gravel, I took great care not to let my candy fall out. I patted my plaid pocket to feel my safety and comfort. Those candy bars would warm me soon.

I could barely make out the trail back to the cabin, and the steps were in darkness when I reached them. I was late, the last girl in the cabin. Taps had been blown and my cabinmates were asleep. Only Debbie Sue read a *Soap Opera Update* on her bed, flashlight clamped under her chin.

"About time, Bets."

"Whoops, am I late? You're not mad, are you Debbie Sue?" I needed to test her mood.

"I will be if you don't get into that bed, kiddo."

I had to keep her talking. It was crucial to find out if she'd heard about the weigh-in. Casually, I sat at the foot of her bed. I crossed my legs. "So what's new Debbie Sue?"

"What's new is that you're going to hop into that sack right now, and I'm going off to the counselors' den."

No. The nurse would be there. She'd tell everyone. All the counselors would laugh at me over Cokes and cigarettes. I had to keep Debbie Sue here and talking.

"What do you guys do down there anyway?"

"What we do we don't tell. Especially to pipsqueaks like you."

Pipsqueak. There was a word I could really identify with. It meant little.

Debbie Sue tossed away her magazine and turned

the flashlight on me. "You know something Bets? Oh forget it. Never mind."

Here it comes, I thought. I didn't want to hear it at all, but I had to. I had to know where I stood. "Come on, what were you going to say?"

"I don't know if I should."

"Try it."

"All right. It may sound silly, but I'm really considering a Hollywood career."

Hollywood. Debbie Sue wanted to talk about Hollywood.

"You know, make a few commercials, then land a small part on *As the World Turns*. I mean I wouldn't want to do soaps forever. Get an agent that would push me. Star in a low budget. Work my way up."

That certainly wasn't the way I'd envisioned it for myself. A few years in off-off Broadway, then whammo, the big time. But she probably didn't want to know my plans. "Hey that's a good idea Debbie Sue. You'd be just great."

"You think so? Sometimes I wonder if I have the looks. It's a rough world out there." She stared off into space as though it were a giant mirror, then remembered me again. "Okay now, get into bed."

I braved the cold sheets and yanked up my extra blanket. Hollywood. I settled into my pillow and my tongue checked over my newly brushed teeth. Pipsqueak. I fondled the Clark Bar, feeling its smooth paper. I ran my finger up and down the Tootsie Roll, then slipped them both under my pillow just like a piece of wedding cake. I was so sleepy. I would

dream about the Hollywood cake. The Hollyclark
cake.

That Clark Bar and Tootsie Roll went into my
trunk, on the bottom under a mustard-colored
sweater too hideous ever to wear. Since I hadn't eaten
them the night before, I thought I might as well put
them in a safe place. Somehow it was exhilarating
just to have candy there—to know it was mine and
secret. Everyone else thought I'd eaten it! I'd played
a grand joke, even on Worm who'd so generously
contributed.

At breakfast I passed the brown sugar jar on
without pause, and sucked tasteless cream of wheat
from my spoon.

"What's wrong with you? Don't you want French
toast?" Worm asked, dribbling on maple syrup.

"Look at that soggy mess. Repulsive."

As soon as we left the table my stomach was alive
with gurglings and rumblings, activated by the sight
of food. Those growlings swashed across me, up and
down like amplified plumbing sounds.

By lunch I was ravenous. I craved a double cheese-
burger with mayonnaise and catsup. I longed for a
bag of potato chips and a quart of chocolate milk.
Use self control dear. Eat sparingly. I gobbled my tuna
sandwich in half-a-dozen bites, but I didn't take
another. *Use self control.* No desserts.

Halfway through supper a bass note sounded deep
in my empty stomach. It bubbled crankily along,
gnashing and grinding under my ribs. *"Hungry!"* it

yelled. I could hardly believe it, my stomach spoke to me, said a real word.

"You got the flu or what?" Worm asked.

"There's just something about this food that turns me off, I don't know."

What a lie. The amount of food that ladened the trestle table was all I'd ever daydreamed. I could have a full plate, finish it, then load up again with, say, the candied sweet potatoes. These tiny lumps I allowed myself were silly jokes. How could I make them last the entire dinner hour?

I picked at a salad the way I'd seen Mother do it. She'd put a carrot round on her fork, then a pepper strip which she'd shake off, reject for being too large, too filling. She'd stab at a small lettuce leaf.

And of course there would have to be fudge-topped brownies for dessert. All day I'd deprived myself with will power I didn't know possible, and then this. Brownies, big and chocolate. I looked at the two on my plate. There was no question: I absolutely must have them. There was no question either that two brownies would wipe out the whole day of dieting and make a good start on the next. There'd be nothing to show for all this pain at the weigh-in next Sunday.

My paper napkin was still in good shape. Worm and the other girls were busy eating. With a fast swipe the brownies slid from my plate to my lap. I tidily wrapped them under the table, sandwiching the fudge. Easy. They were ready to go under the mustard sweater in the trunk.

"Posture perfect, posture perfect
Do not slump! Do not slump!

Straighter you must sit up
Straighter you must sit up
Hide that hump.
Hide that hump."

Actually, there were other things I planned to hide. Some humps were made of backbone and skinny shoulder blades, which could be easily hidden. My own hump felt thick like a water buffalo, and that I would never be able to hide. That simply would have to disappear. I would hide my sweets.

7 ✷ Discovering Beauty

"**W**ho do you think will be Beauty this year?" Anna Banana asked as she caught up to me on the path.

That was a strange question. I was dawdling my way to the lodge, moving slow as a dog to a flea bath. I was in no hurry for another tiny supper full of torment. Around me were gaggles of campers all headed cheerfully for another meal. Now here was Anna talking gibberish.

"Who do I think will be what?"

"Beauty. B-E-A-U-T-Y."

I said nothing. Wait, my inner voice told me. Don't make a fool of yourself.

"Lolly Sharp was Beauty last year, you know," Anna whispered.

Lolly was walking ahead of us. Her posture was perfect. A thick, gleaming braid swung and bounced against her back. Her small waist was circled by a Mexican silver belt. Her legs were long, finely shaped. It was certainly no news to me that Lolly was a beauty.

"It's a good thing she can't be Beauty two years in a row. Those are the rules."

That was crazy. Lolly would be a beauty for the rest of her life. She'd been one since she was born. I saw her floating in a bubble of charm and luck, like the good witch of Oz. I looked at her now, walking with friends who bumped her shoulders, pressed close and touched her arm for attention—anything to stay within her magic. I knew how they felt, because I felt exactly the same way when we clasped hands for the buddy count at swimming lessons. Since Lolly was a beauty, and would be that way not just two years in a row but forever, there must be more to this than I knew.

Reluctantly, I broke our silence. "What do you mean two years in a row?"

"The contest, dummy, the contest." Anna looked at me with superior puzzlement.

I'd been told and still I knew nothing. What contest? Some sort of beauty contest? I had to find out more.

After supper I headed for the Brown. Long before it came in sight a powerful smell invaded the trail. It was a busy evening there, wooden doors banging, splintered along their hinges from being slammed. Respectful of the stench, campers hung back along the edge of the woods waiting for their turn. I was told the chemical stink was useful for covering up an after-dinner cigarette. I made it a point to stay away at that hour, since I was always afraid Louise would force another Marlboro on me. Campers came slamming out, hitching up their shorts and fanning the air like windshield wipers in a thunderstorm.

I entered a stall and crouched on the seat with my

nostrils pinched. I breathed down my throat, mouth open. I took my time, waited to hear a few more doors bang, then yelled out, "Hey! Who knows when the contest is?" My voice was huskier than usual. It seemed like a good disguise.

"Which one?" someone yelled back.

Now there was something to puzzle over. How could there be more than one contest?

"The Beauty Contest?" I tried.

"Final week, same as always. Saturday afternoon before we sail the Wishing Boats," hollered a voice from my left.

That was it. A beauty contest.

"How do you get in it?"

"Get picked by your cabin," the girl shouted, as though I had every right to ask. As though I could be a contestant.

"Check," I yelled, closing the conversation.

I waited for enough slams to feel I probably wouldn't be identified by my unknown advisor as I came out, then left the putrid Brown. I took a trail to the cabin.

Of course I'd never be chosen. Impossible even to dream of such a thing—but . . . But what if I lost lots of weight on this diet I seemed to be on? Then could I be in it? No. You had to be beautiful to be in a beauty contest. I wasn't beautiful—yet. Maybe I never would be. But somehow, in a way I didn't understand, this contest was terribly important to me. I had to know every detail of what would happen.

Would it be like the Miss America contest? I'd watched that every year on TV. Would they wear ball gowns? That was nuts, no camper had anything like that. I saw them unpacking.

Debbie Sue might. Yes, Debbie Sue would have a long, formal gown of orchid silk that fell in layers from her tiny waist, strapless, with sequins outlining the heart-shaped bodice. She'd have satin shoes dyed to match, with thin heels that peeked out under her skirt as she swished across the stage. In her gorgeous hair a diamond tiara would shower back the lights like a thousand prisms.

Could that Beauty, that great Beauty, be, not Debbie Sue—but me? Could that be my own face smiling, my own hand waving to the crowd? After a few pounds? Maybe?

I heard footsteps on the pine needles behind me and sprinted to the cabin. I arrived breathless, with a running pain under my ribs.

Debbie Sue was there, spreading out clothing on her bed. Her jaws smacked together, then separated sideways while loud clicks bubbled from her teeth.

"Don't tell anyone you saw this," Debbie Sue said. She pulled a hunk of gray gum from her mouth and wrapped it in silver paper. "Miss Mack would explode if she found me with gum. She hates gum more than anything."

"More than she hates slouchers?" We both laughed.

"Hey Bets, you came along at just the right time."

That's what I thought—to find Debbie Sue alone was real luck.

"Tell me the truth now."

She knew about the weigh-in! She knew about the diet!

"Does this Italian boatman's top go with my blue shorts?" She draped a striped shirt over her shoulders, anchored it with her chin, and pushed it in at the waist. "Tomorrow's my day off and I'm going to town. Be honest now, what do you think?" She practiced her smile on me, holding the shirt, swiveling from side to side.

"Great Debbie Sue. It looks great. Now I have an important question to ask you."

"Go ahead, kiddo. I'm all yours."

"Please tell me everything I should know about the Bathing Beauty Contest."

Debbie Sue brought a green cardigan from her trunk. "Well, do you think it clashes?" She held a corner of the sweater against the shirt.

"It looks real nice, Debbie Sue." I sighed.

"Or maybe I should chuck them both and wear the pink shirt with the white-on-white monogrammed sweater. What do you think?"

I thought I'd cry if Debbie Sue didn't tell me about the contest quickly, before the other campers came in.

"Come on Debbie Sue," I begged, "I'm new this year. I don't know anything about the contest and everyone else does. Who'll tell me if you won't?"

At last I had her attention. The pivoting halted. Debbie Sue squeaked down on the metal bed hard, making a book bounce to the floor. When the jiggling stopped, she thumped a pillow behind her back, kicked off her sandals, and stretched her long legs to the iron bed-foot. She looked down at me, sitting cross-legged on the floor.

"You're going to love it Bets."

"Why? What happens? What's it like? Who's in it?" I spoke so fast it sounded like one question.

Debbie Sue gazed out the window a few seconds, then began to drawl, giving each word time and weight. "Everyone looks beautiful, just beautiful. Of course us counselors help with make-up—eye shadow in the crease only, a line of blush right along the cheek bone." She reached over, traced a line under my eye from nose to temple. "Some mascara to thicken up the lashes, set the eyes off better. You know, that sort of thing." She looked more distant. "Then we style the hair—cut, shape, tease, curl. You know, get it just perfect."

Just perfect. I ran my hand over my hair. It would take work, but it wasn't impossible. We were silent.

"I swear," Debbie Sue shook her head, "it's the hardest thing to decide."

Decide? How she could make my hair just perfect? Cut it in shingled layers perhaps? Hold it back from my ears with combs?

"Decide what?" I finally asked.

"Why, the winner!" Debbie Sue said, surprised.

Ah yes, I thought. If this was a contest there must be a winner.

"So who does it? Who decides?" I asked.

"Miss Mack and Dusty, silly." She blinked hard, or maybe she winked. "Honestly, didn't you know that?"

Could this be true? What kind of beauty standards could Miss Mack have, when she'd wear high-tops and bicycle shorts? Miss Mack would judge a beauty contest? No. And Dusty? That didn't make sense even

if he was the only man at Camp Sunny Days. I
pictured his one eye, busy sizing all the girls up and
down and side to side, while the glass one stared
straight ahead. Would he really be in charge?

"This is Miss Mack's baby—the pride of her summer. It was her idea years and years ago. She's the
one who awards the prize, so naturally she's the
judge. And Dusty would never give up the chance of
a free, long ogle."

"Tell me what the prize is, Debbie Sue." I was
almost sure I knew. I watched her mouth as she
started to speak, lips precise over her white teeth.

"First, the winner has her picture taken for Miss
Mack's collection of Beauties. The one she has on her
cabin wall."

I'd never heard of this collection.

"Then there's a tour of Lake Sunset with Dusty in
his patrol boat, at full speed!"

"Oh." I sighed my disappointment. This wasn't
what I'd dreamed of, a ride in the patrol boat with
creepy Dusty.

"And here it comes, Bets. Candy bars. A big grab
bag full for the whole cabin. A grocery sack stuffed
to the top with all kinds."

Wow. So that was it, even more than I'd dared
think.

"That means we have to pick our best girl, because
the whole cabin's a winner!"

I could see the gorge, late at night: Caramel stuck
to my teeth, coconut lodged between them. Chocolate
dribbling over the edge of my lips. The cabin floor
would be slippery with wrappers; my cabinmates full,

delirious because I, the winner, had brought them. Debbie Sue was quiet, as lost in reverie as I was. But there was more I had to learn.

"What do they wear?"

Debbie Sue lowered her head, peering at me as though I'd asked something very dumb indeed. I squirmed, and she gave me a forgiving smile. Perhaps she thought she was dealing with a real hick, someone who'd never seen a beauty contest before.

"I mean in Miss America they wear ball gowns after the talent judging," I explained. I wanted her to know I was up on it all.

"That would be pretty hard here since no one brings formals, dopey. We just do the swim suit division."

Swim suit, dopey. I was lucky no one else had come in. I'd ask the next question quickly.

"Just when do you pick who will be in it?" I dreaded the answer.

"You guys do that. There's lots of time, it's not till the end of camp. Whenever."

Debbie Sue couldn't realize how important "whenever" was.

If it wasn't until the end of camp I could be thin. Surely I could lose thirty, forty, even fifty pounds if I tried hard enough. And if my pain was any measure, I was trying hard enough. But if they were to choose their Bathing Beauty tomorrow, it would never be me. What I needed was time. To get skinny. To clear up a red bump swelling on my chin. To try my hair in different ways. To work on my posture.

Could I really do all that in seven weeks? I could

try harder than I'd ever tried anything. Or should I simply stop dreaming of being Miss Bathing Beauty and think about which girl had the best chance from the cabin? After all, that candy prize would be shared.

Debbie Sue flipped over on her stomach; she licked her thumb, pushed the corner of a *Vogue* magazine. I'd lost her attention.

"Anything else Debbie Sue?"

"Huh?" she grunted. Suddenly she swung her legs over, turned to sitting in one sweep. "Look at this fantastic coat. All that white fur, and a hood. Oh Bets, wouldn't that look divine on me?"

I scrambled to look. The coat Debbie Sue had chosen from Fabulous Fall Fashions was perfect. It would cuddle her small self, curl around her like a bunny rabbit, and frame her chiseled face. Debbie Sue yanked her blanket from the bed, draped it over her head and made moon-eyes at me.

"Super Debbie Sue. It looks perfect on you." I was going to try once more. "Is there anything else to tell me? Do I know everything now?"

"About what?"

"The contest."

"Oh yeah." She held the magazine at arm's length, then brought it slowly toward her face to see how the coat would look approaching from a distance. She put it down at last, and stared from her bed.

"Well," she said thoughtfully, her mind on me again. "There's another way to win the same prize. It's called the Ugly contest."

8 ✳ A Member of the Chosen Few

The second Sunday I was prepared for the weigh-in. I skipped breakfast. At the end of one long week of dieting, there was no way I could have refused a pitcher of maple syrup or a hunk of butter.

I did go to Sunday dinner though, in my white uniform like everyone else—but this week I thought we all looked more like geese than swans. I nibbled a drumstick because I didn't think it was fattening. I found that if I pushed my gravy around in the mashed potatoes it made a mud pie so unappetizing I didn't want it.

"Seconds?" Worm inquired.

"Just pass the green beans," I answered listlessly.

"Hey, you're not turning into a veggie are you? That would be too much, really."

"Do me a favor, Worm. Ask no questions."

And that's the kind of friend Worm was. She didn't say another word, although I'm sure she knew what was going on. She pretended everything was absolutely normal.

Anna Banana sat on my other side. "Would you look at what dessert is? I can't believe my eyeballs! Cream puffs!"

A cream puff. That would be a mess in my napkin; I'd never get it to my trunk.

"Who wants an extra?" I asked, not really believing it was my own voice. "Someone go ahead and take it. My stomach aches."

It did rather, a tight hungry burn.

I hurried along the path to the infirmary. This time I moved fast because there were no surprises ahead. I tried to convince myself I wasn't frightened of Miss Mack, the nurse, or the scale. I knew I was thinner. I felt lighter. Empty. I must not only weigh less, I must look smaller too. When you try that hard it shows—it's got to. My father was forever telling me, "Hard work always pays off." Of course he was talking about my math homework, but it must be true with diets, too.

"Can you believe we're going through this same jackass business again?" I asked Worm, plunking down beside her on the grass.

"Every week till the end of summer."

Yes, everything was the same white—campers, nurse, scale. Only Miss Mack looked waxy yellow.

"What's with Miss Mack? Don't you think her skin looks like parchment paper?" I kept my voice low.

"I think it gets that way from sunbathing too much.

Or using Q.T. or something. That's what it must be—" she nodded wisely—"chemicals."

Worm's name was called and she was up and back in a flash. Now it would be only a few minutes before the truth of the scale. Miss Mack would be so startled to see how much I'd lost. Maybe she'd offer public congratulations. And maybe she'd write to Mother. *Dear Mrs. Sherman, Your amazing daughter has more will power than anyone I've ever met.*

"Shaw, Patty."

In fact, could it be Miss Mack would even let me out of future weigh-ins?

I was next.

"Sherman." Miss Mack's eyes didn't leave the list, but her mouth formed the word clearly.

The wooden steps creaked under me, then I was on the porch. This was it. At last I'd prove what I could do. Shoes on, I mounted the scale. No embarrassment, no asking for special favors. I looked out over the campers, and when I saw Louise, I smiled.

The nurse fumbled with the balance, pushing, tapping. I stood very still. But my calm self-confidence began to tremble. There was nothing to be nervous about, I assured myself. I'd done a fabulous job this week.

"Sherman," the nurse rasped. "142½ pounds."

The numbers seemed to echo from a great distance. I wasn't sure I'd heard correctly. 142½ pounds? What did that mean? As I left the scale—confused—something gripped my insides and shook my whole body. I heard someone moan, "Oh no." It was my own voice. One week of hunger and pain. One solid week without joy and I had lost only a pound and a half. It had been worth nothing.

Miss Mack dismissed me without a word, calling the next name. I slunk off the porch. I had to be alone, there was no way I could return even to Worm. I hugged the infirmary wall, turned the corner, and slid down onto the damp grass.

How could I go on? I should have lost five pounds, three at the very least. I'd tortured myself for nothing. A lousy pound and a half. Now I felt no thinner— that was self-delusion a few minutes ago. The elastic in my white shorts stretched just as much and my hips were still lumpy. Worse, the top roll of my stomach was still the same size as my breasts. I bent over and grabbed it, pinching hard. Why couldn't I carve off fat with a knife? Take that horrible roll in my hand, cut it and throw it away?

How could I be a Bathing Beauty looking this way?

Never. That was the answer, never. There was only one thing that could help. My trunk, its corner of pleasure. Waiting for me. I knew all that saving had been about something. That would be my consolation. Everyone was still at the weigh-in; the cabin would be empty now. I could sneak away, take the trail to the Brown, then double back to the cabin. I'd have time. And I'd only eat those old brownies, that's all.

I heaved to my feet and rubbed at the grass stains on my Sunday shorts. Taking care to walk quietly over the leaves and twigs, I began the uphill trudge to the Brown.

"Betsy," a voice hissed behind me. "Wait up, Betsy."

I turned. Lolly Sharp—the beauty, the sleek one—

caught up with me. Lolly'd spoken to me only on the beach during buddy checks and safety lessons. She'd given me the high sign now and then in the lodge, but that was it. I'd envied the girls who walked with her. Now was my chance and I didn't want it.

"I know where you're going," Lolly cooed.

Impossible. Unless Lolly knew a fat girl would be sneaking off for only one reason. To fill her gut.

"You couldn't have the foggiest idea where I'm going." I heard my voice frosty and menacing, like Louise. I actually felt proud I could be bitchy to one of the most popular girls.

"Don't be a nincompoop! There's nothing to worry about. I have mine too!"

"You have your what?"

Lolly pulled a cigarette and matches from her shorts pocket. "You see? I did know. Come on, let's hurry."

The relief I felt was so total I wouldn't even contest the nincompoop label. I stumbled up the hill to the smelly Brown behind Lolly. She headed for the end stall.

"You take the other end and give the hawk cry if anyone comes up the path."

I sat on the wooden box in what I thought of as Brown Breathing Position—nostrils crinkled up hard, sucking air over my exposed front teeth. There wouldn't be time to go to the cabin now. Anyway, who could think about eating candy in this horrible place? Oh Lolly, I thought, you may be pretty and popular but you sure are a dodo to put yourself through this for a cigarette.

"Hey Betsy. You done?" Lolly called.

"Almost. In a second," I stage-whispered. "Just one more drag." I figured that made it sound authentic.

"Now let's get out of here!" Lolly bolted from the stall, ran across the clearing, and stopped at a trail that led toward Lake Sunset. It wasn't the one to the infirmary.

"Don't you think we should get back to the weigh-in?" I asked. "They're going to miss us there."

"No way. Once they've got your precious weight, they quit counting. Now Miss Mack's just leading camp songs."

The look on Lolly's face was so wry, with her mouth tightened up on one side and eyes narrowed, that I took a chance. I began to bounce on my toes and with my shoulders absurdly back, arms pinned to my side, I imitated Miss Mack's floppy-handed conducting.

"Heavens praise, heavens praise,
We are the girls from Sunny Days.
We don't smoke and we don't chew
And we don't go out with the boys who do."

"You look just like her!" Lolly snorted.

"I practice in my basement at night," I said modestly.

"I have an idea. You want to see something from the secret life of Miss Mack?" Lolly's voice was breathy with danger. "Of course you do. Follow me."

Of course I didn't. "Wait a minute. Where are you going? I'm not real anxious to get in trouble."

"Nothing to worry about, take it from an old-timer.

They're all going to be singing away for another twenty minutes. You'll be gassed by what I'm going to show you, believe me."

I was skeptical, but I found myself following Lolly—and I had to remind myself this was *the* Lolly Sharp—down a narrow, dusty trail toward the lake. I had no idea where we were going, but for some reason I trusted her.

"I used to wonder why I do it," Lolly said from nothing.

"Do what?" I said to her back.

"Smoke in the Brown. It's such a terrible place to sit, and I really don't like to smoke much."

I looked at Lolly walking, dangles from her Mexican belt bumping out a soft tinkle against her side like chimes, her satiny thick braid swishing across her back with each step. Could there really be anything she didn't much like to do? Wouldn't even the Brown smell like tangerines to a girl like that?

"But now I know why I do it," Lolly continued. "It's because there's really no other way to be alone. I mean there's always someone after you to go here or there. Sometimes it's the only way to get away from them."

"Why did you tell me to wait for you then?"

"Oh you're different, I can tell. You don't need all the gobbledygook everyone else does. I mean I don't even know you, but somehow I don't feel a lot of pressure from you. Hey, look. We're here." Lolly sounded awed, as though she was in the presence of something great and special.

I didn't see anything so spectacular. In a clearing,

on a small bluff overlooking Lake Sunset, was a log cabin, much like the other cabins that dotted Camp Sunny Days. White curtains framed the windows, and an arbor arched over the door, holding up pink, rambling roses.

"Well?" Lolly said.

"Well?"

"This is Miss Mack's own private cabin."

"Looks okay to me."

"You haven't seen the inside yet."

"How are we going to do that?" Somehow I couldn't imagine the two of us picking locks.

"For openers, you can get a pretty good view this way. Come around here, but walk carefully. Try not to leave footprints."

Lolly tiptoed right up to the window next to the door, cupped her hands to her eyes to keep out reflected light, and leaned her nose on the pane. She looked long enough for me to begin counting one hippopotamus.

"Pretty stunning, I'll tell you."

"Let me have a look then."

"You know what you're looking for?"

"How could I?"

"It's the Bathing Beauties, all of them."

I nudged Lolly aside, my shoulder touching hers. Nothing magic rubbed off. Making a tunnel for my eyes with my hands, I peered in Miss Mack's window.

Across the narrow room was an entire wall of photographs, each in an elaborate gold frame. And in the center of every picture was a girl with a banner across her chest. A couple of them had on funny, draped, knee-length bathing suits that looked older than the invention of the camera. There was one in a leopard-skin suit with a claw on her shoulder. Another wore a spiked crown and had an American flag behind her. One seemed to be growing out of a huge seashell.

"What's this all about?" I asked, turning from the window back to Lolly.

"I wondered the same thing when I first saw them. But then it all began to make sense. Miss Mack's the one who started the whole bathing contest idea, right? Well, I think she must have been in one sometime in her life. And these must be people who did the same thing."

"Come off it. Miss Frankenstein America is the only possibility for Miss Mack."

"Come around to the back window, I'll show you something else," Lolly said, her voice dropping back down to a whisper.

Behind the cabin we pushed aside brambly roses, touching them carefully between prickers. Pulling our knees high, we stepped gingerly to the window. This time I looked first.

It was a bathroom, but not like any bathroom you'd expect in a log cabin. It had mirrors floor to ceiling on one wall, and a funny old-fashioned hair drier that looked like a motorcycle helmet on a stand.

"I thought we weren't supposed to have electricity here," I said.

"Miss Mack can have whatever she wants," Lolly said behind me.

"So that's what accounts for the manicotti hairdo."

Staring into the mirror was an exercycle; Mother had one of those, but she got tired of it and now it lived in the basement with my outgrown bikes. Miss Mack's shelves sagged under tubes, bottles, jars, and boxes of perms and dyes. A pair of rubber gloves were draped lifeless in the sink. There was a black lump in the soap dish. It all made me feel sweaty and a little weak.

"She's really into it, huh?" Lolly started picking her way back out through the roses. "It fascinates me how she could go so far in that direction."

It fascinated me that I was hearing this from Lolly Sharp, former Camp Sunny Days Beauty Queen. It seemed she had gone about as far in the beauty direction as anyone.

"Now I'm going to show you something else, and this is the icing on the cake, the cherry on the fudge sundae—I promise."

She led me around to the third side of the log cabin, and marched right up to the window. "Watch this." With one hand she banged the window sash, and with the other she pushed up. Like lightning the window was open and Lolly was halfway through it, her legs and feet scrambling in the air. I heard a thud and she disappeared completely.

"Come on, Betsy," she hissed, her head popping up inside the cabin. "If you get a running start it'll be easier."

Without thinking about the consequences—the fact that this was breaking and entering—I did; leapt up on the windowsill better than I'd ever mounted a horse, and eased myself to the other side without a hitch. I was in Miss Mack's kitchen.

It was tidy as could be; not a plate was in the sink, not a pot on the stove. In fact, I couldn't imagine when Miss Mack would ever use a stove, since she ate all three meals in the lodge with us. I checked out the fridge. There was a half-used bottle of catsup, that's all.

"Okay Lolly. So you've brought me to an empty kitchen. Now let's get out of here before we get caught."

"Wait a second. I promised cherries and I plan to deliver." She reached up and opened one of the yellow metal cabinets above the sink. She took down a tufted, white satin box. "Voilà, Mademoiselle," she said, bowing low.

I knew exactly what it was before I took off the puffy white lid. There were chocolate nuggets nestled inside, each in pleated brown paper.

"Wow."

"And this isn't all. These cabinets are filled with candy. Didn't she secretly give you a piece when you first came? It's one of her big thrills, you know. She thinks she's got everybody's number by doing that."

She sure had mine. So it wasn't me she especially wanted to make friends with. It was just her way of passing herself around.

"She'd never miss a few of these," Lolly said. "Grab some and let's beat it back to camp. The weigh-in's probably over about now." She scooped up a handful.

I examined each piece. Eager as I was to get out of there, I wanted to pick exactly the right ones. Each was crowned by a chocolate curlicue, but I wasn't fooled. I knew which would be golden brittle, which would have runny cherry filling, which would hold sharp mint. I lifted three out delicately by their skirts.

Lolly took one and held it up to the window as though she was trying to read a letter through its envelope. "Caramel. That's all I like. Let me find a few more." She ate the caramel as only a thin girl can—in mincy bites—and rummaged through the box. "Got 'em. Let's go."

She put the lid on, pressing down the edges.

"Hey look!" I cried. We both stared at the box.

Lolly had left two precise, chocolate thumbprints on the white satin top.

"That's enough to convict me. Quick, we have to clean them off."

"Where's the sponge?" I ran over to the sink. Nothing.

"She'll be back any minute. We've got to get out of here. Let's just put it away." Lolly's voice was desperate.

But I already had my shirt out of my shorts, had undone the bottom buttons, and was wetting down the shirt tails in the sink. At least there was water.

"Hurry Betsy!"

I smeared the prints with one side of my shirt, and tried to erase the smudge with the other side. The satin box top now had two brown streaks. It was the best I could do.

"Let's move it!" She stuffed the box in the cabinet and slammed the door.

I grabbed my candy from the table. Awkwardly I crawled back out the window, one hand a claw of chocolate.

"It's death to us if we're ever caught—you're aware of that, aren't you?" Lolly said.

"I wish you wouldn't use those words—I feel pretty scared about this already. Miss Mack's going to know someone's been in there, and that's for sure."

"Just keep it our secret. There's no way she can find out who it was, and there's no way she'd suspect me. Now follow me. I'll show you a shortcut and we can walk back by the beach. We'll take off our shoes and walk in the water—no one will know where we've come from."

We splashed through the riplets that touched the shore, taking care not to let our feet bump the weeds hiding darkly in the water. Lolly casually ate another candy. The hot afternoon sun made me long for a swim. I held my candy carefully so as not to melt it any more than it was. A mosquito buzzed in the distance, then roared louder and louder.

"Oh brother. Look who's after us," Lolly said shading her eyes as she looked into the horizon. Dusty's patrol boat swept down on us. It made a last-second turn to avoid being grounded, the way skiers turn sharply to stop, sending up spray. He cut the engine.

I tucked my shirt back in my shorts. "Quick!" I whispered to Lolly. "Get rid of your candy!" I dropped mine in the deep front pocket of my white shorts. Lolly's last piece went into her mouth.

"Hey! Hey you girls! Just where've you been? What do you think you're doing?"

This is it, I thought. It's all over. I knew there was nothing Lolly could say with her teeth glued together. But I took a deep breath and heard myself shout out to the boat, "After the weigh-in we went for a walk. Anything wrong with that? Look, we're buddies." I grabbed Lolly's hand, now empty of chocolate, and held it high. "You don't need to worry about us and waterfront safety!"

Dusty looked at us doubtfully—I could tell by the way his mouth hung open. He knew something else had gone on, but he had no evidence. The crime hadn't been uncovered.

"You girls get on back with everyone else now, understand? I don't want to catch you back down here again." He gave no sign of knowing Lolly, though he'd carried her on his back in the fireman's carry, and she must have ridden in his motorboat last year as the beauty queen. "Get a move on it now. I'm not budging until I see you girls back in camp."

Obediently we jogged down the beach to the waterfront, then ran through the birches that separated it from Camp Sunny Days.

"We were lucky," I panted. "If he'd come any sooner he'd have seen where we were coming from."

"He'd have caught us with the goods, too. You were amazing, Betsy. I never heard anyone sound so innocent in my life. Let's get back to our cabins, and we'll never say another word about this, even to each other." She turned away, then swung back. "You know what I think?" She put her hand on my shoulder and snapped my bra strap through my shirt. "I think you're really terrific."

I'm really terrific, I'm really terrific, I thought on my way back to the cabin. That's right—I even lost a pound and a half in the first week of my diet. I've got a pocketful of candy, and I'm not going to eat it.

"So where have you been Miss Bets? Out practicing to be a juvenile delinquent?" Debbie Sue asked as I came in the cabin. She was sitting on her bed, with my cabinmates draped around her like a mink stole. They all looked up at me.

"Out for a little walk on the beach, that's all." I had to turn my back and hope they wouldn't notice my ears were red. I longed to tell them I'd been with Lolly Sharp, but I'd promised to say nothing. And I was counting on Dusty to forget about us. If he hadn't recognized Lolly, he surely wouldn't know who I was.

"You're going to have to be on time, kiddo. Now come on over here and take a gander at what we're looking at."

Debbie had her scrapbook out. It bulged with pressed flowers—gardenias turned from cream to brown, and orchids with the palest ghost of purple.

"I wore this corsage to the Delta Sig Mid-winter Madness Ball," Debbie Sue said smugly, pointing to a mashed cluster of baby roses. "And look!"

I squeezed closer to see those pages, and felt my hip jam against Julia's shoulder. Whoops, a chocolate crust gave way. I could just imagine what the inside of my pocket looked like.

"Here's the carnation I sent my date for the Leap Year Dance. Imagine! Me! Sending flowers to a guy! But I told him it was just a loan, I'd have to have it back at the end of the dance for my scrapbook. Remember that next leap year, girls."

I had to get that candy out of my pocket and under the mustard-colored sweater.

As Debbie Sue began singing her favorite song, I inched toward my treasure chest.

> "Kappa Kappa Gamma
> I'm so glad I ama
> Member of the chosen few. . . ."

"You see that lock of hair? Hey! Come back over here, Bets! How can you see anything across the room?"

I went over to the bed, but I didn't stand too near this time. My nose was filled with that sweet chocolate scent—I didn't want them to get a whiff of it.

"Now that lock of hair's very important, 'cause that's just a part of what happened to one Zeta Beta when we got ahold of him. And that's one thing that frat won't try again—a panty raid."

"What's that?" Dede asked. "It sounds dirty."

"It sounds just like it is. Those boys think they can get away with anything—breaking in at night, yelling and whooping, ripping through your drawers to steal your underthings."

"Why would they do that, Debbie Sue?" I was dumbfounded. Why would anyone want underpants?

"They hang them out the window of the frat house like flags to show what big men they are."

I shuddered. No one better ever panty raid me.

"But that's the last time they'll ever get my bra. A dozen girls—especially Kappa Kappa Gammas—and a pair of scissors can do wonders on a Zeta. We gave him a Mohawk and there's the proof!" She pointed to the hair and slammed the scrapbook shut for emphasis.

I felt the crushed candy pooling in the bottom of my pocket. What if it oozed down my leg? I had to get it out of there.

From her trunk Debbie Sue took a glittery, streamer-tipped baton. "The High Flingers! The world's greatest majorettes," she announced proudly. "We lead the famous Iowa bagpipe band around the football stadium at half time."

I backed off from the admiring group and sat on my little iron bed.

Debbie Sue stretched, strutting up and down the cabin, leapt on her trunk, twirled the baton behind her back and under her leg. She swaggered around, marching knee to chin, back arched.

As I watched, safe in my corner, I suddenly yearned to be like Debbie Sue. My brain knew this was nonsense. I hadn't been brought up to be a cheerleader, and I'd never wanted to be one. If Mother could see Debbie Sue prancing and parading, she'd say, "Really, Dear, how crass." But my heart wouldn't agree with my brain, and beat faster to prove it. I knew in a terrible and important way, if I could have strutted and danced and flaunted myself like that I'd never have been excluded from the block club. It might have changed my life.

Triumphantly the baton spun and dipped. Debbie Sue sank effortlessly into a split on the floor, like a broken clothespin.

Even Worm was awed. "Go Debbie Sue," she shrieked, and blew a whistle through her fingers.

Like a launched rocket, Worm's whistle pierced the

barrier between my head and heart. My past whirled behind me. I ached to be like Debbie Sue. I must. I'd make a scrapbook like hers. Please, let me be a member of the chosen few. Lolly Sharp would be my best friend, and everyone would know it. My hair would be long, a sheet of silk floating behind me. I'd learn a split, no matter how it hurt.

It was more important than ever to get that candy in my trunk and not in my mouth. I was going to be a Beauty. I'd never tell Debbie Sue or Lolly or the Fivers I was on a diet. This was my problem alone, and I had no intention of letting it flap in the wind like a bra from a fraternity window.

9 ✳ Getting Noticed

I lost weight.

Four weeks later I no longer had a red rippled waist from my elastic shorts' bands. My hand mirror told me I'd shrunk my cheeks and most of my double chin. There was less of a flesh bubble looping out between my arm and bathing suit strap. I was definitely thinner.

But I had not become less hungry.

Breakfast, lunch, supper—each was another test to pass. Could I eat slowly enough? Were my bites tiny enough? Though my meals were dreary, I somehow grew fond of them. There was a secret kernel of pleasure in this torture, like the block club initiation—the sting of gravel in my knees proved I'd dared to jump. Now that the diet had taken over, it was such a large part of my life I'd miss it if I stopped. Hunger became a friend.

There was great progress in my treasure chest. The inside of my trunk was a jumble of clothing, but at the bottom, under the mustard sweater, my sweet collection grew as steadily as Grandmother's roses under mulch. I checked my hoardings daily, hovering like a giant thundercloud over the trunk. Those first candy bars had been so hard to come by, but now they multiplied like bright silk scarves from a magician's hat. I could count my victories. I needed them to prove exactly what it was I hadn't eaten—which in turn proved I was getting thinner. I needed evidence I was changing.

Because no one else noticed.

Since I'd wanted so much to fit in with the other girls, I'd gone out of my way not to call special attention to myself. But now no one noticed I was thinner. Worm might have, but I'd discouraged her from talking about size from the beginning. It was too depressing that I weighed so much and she weighed so little. Now I found myself waiting for someone to tell me how much better I looked. They said nothing. I waited for someone to notice my clothes were no longer tight. No one did.

At the weigh-in, where every week my weight was lower by several pounds, I desperately wanted Miss Mack to say something. Perhaps just pat me secretly, or whisper that I was doing well. Nothing.

Nothing anywhere, from anyone. It seemed it would take more than losing weight to do the trick. I had to make more changes—immediately—so they could see who I really was.

I knew the next step. All the Beauties did it. I'd have to learn the mysteries of the razor.

"Better line up deodorant," Jolee warned as we

shuffled through the woods to the dips side of Lake Sunset.

"Why?" It embarrassed me how little I knew. Sometimes I felt as out of touch as Mother.

"Once you start shaving your pits you'll need it every day."

"That's right, ding-a-ling. You'll stink if you don't use it," Wanda chimed in.

I did want to join the Beauties, the shavers. Yet I didn't know exactly what it would mean; certainly I'd never thought of deodorant before. I'd recently become rather fascinated by my underarm smells—strong, sour, secretly not unpleasant. Sometimes alone, I'd put my nose into my armpit and take a big sniff.

"You'll never get a boyfriend if you smell like the inside of your tennis shoes," Jolee said, flicking her towel. We neared the lake, walking through dawn-cold woods. "It's not just the smell," she continued. "I mean can you think of anything more disgusting than a woman with a hairy armpit?"

Truth was I also liked the grove of new light hairs that had sprouted in my hollow. I'd waited a long time for them. I did want to shave, but I was nervous about losing those baby, silky hairs. Mother had said when I started shaving, my skin would turn prickly and the hair would grow in black and wiry.

"I mean it would be like growing a beard under your arms," Dede cackled from behind.

That did it.

I put my shampoo, soap container, and towel on the wobbly dock that limped out into Lake Sunset.

Here was our privacy, on the dips side of the lake, away from the swimming area, and Dusty's patrol boat.

"Ye gods it's cold!" Wanda cried as she took off her robe. "Am I ever brave!"

I yanked my warm flannel pajama top over my head. As I stepped out of my pajama bottoms, I hugged myself for an instant and rubbed off the rawness.

I looked around and saw them all naked. Against the early morning sky I saw them flat and round, triangle fuzzed and hairless, bony and lumpy.

"What are you looking at, girl?" Wanda asked.

Quickly my toes curled on the dock end and my body pushed through the air. I disappeared under the shocking water, then came up shrieking.

I stood waist deep next to the dock, shampooing with dozens of other girls. As I scrubbed my scalp, I heard a giggle which could only be Lolly Sharp's.

I turned. Every chance to be near her now was wonderful. Since our escapade there was a secret between us.

Lolly pulled her foamy hair into a stiff peak, curving it over into a curl. "I'm Madame de Pompadour."

"Yeah, Lolly. And do you know who Betsy-babes is?" The voice was unmistakably Louise's. "If you're Madame de Pompadour, then our Betsy-babes is Marie Antoinette, that's who she is."

That sounded okay. I'd always thought Marie Antoinette heroic in the face of death. But Louise's smirk made me nervous.

"You know why?"

"Why?" Lolly said.

I looked down at the water ripples and made little waves with my fingers.

"You don't know why? Because when they cut off her head she lost ten pounds of ugly fat!"

I didn't wait to hear if Lolly laughed—I couldn't bear that. If she was going to betray me, I didn't want to be around for it. I breaststroked fiercely under water, blowing air bubbles to clear the shampoo streaming from my hair. I surfaced on the other side of the dock next to the shavers.

Debbie Sue was there, standing one-legged in the shallow water. Her other leg was hoisted on the dock, and she bent over it like a ballerina doing stretches. I watched her press a mound of lather in her hand and spread it ankle to knee, leaving little white meringue peaks. Then her razor came up smooth and free, shaving, skimming, until all her tanned leg was showing.

How would I ever learn to do that? I could see myself—a patchwork quilt of Band-Aids. But I had to try.

"Can I borrow that, Debbie Sue?" It was nervy to ask—Mother always said a razor was as personal as a toothbrush.

"Sure, kiddo, about time you got into this. Going to take some shadow from those gams?"

"I've never done it before."

"Nothing to it." Debbie Sue squirted foam in my palm.

I put my foot on the dock. "Alert the hospital," I

said as the razor made its first run to my knee. "Have a transfusion ready."

"You got it Babycakes. That's it. What did I tell you?" She swam away.

Debbie Sue was right; it was easy. I scraped the gentle fuzz from my legs. And it wasn't so hard to stand naked with these girls, either. No one paid special attention.

The water near me trembled and foamed. Louise broke through the surface.

"Think you're a big shot now, huh Betsy-babes?" she sneered, shaking water off her curls. "One of the in crowd? Lolly's pal?"

I dabbed lather in my armpit.

"Just because a Bathing Beauty's taken a shine to you, you think you got it made?"

"My goodness, why are you so jealous?"

"Uh-oh. Wouldn't get too big mouthed or too cocky if I were you. There's a choosing a-coming, you know. Don't say I didn't warn you."

A choosing. For the contest. Of course I knew, that's why I was doing all this. I turned my back on Louise and shaved under my arms.

"Worm, have you noticed anything different about me?"

"Different? Let me think. You eat more vegetables. And—oh yes—you've grown a second nose." Worm touched my forehead.

"Seriously. Pass the beets, will you?"

"Well, seriously, I can't say that I have. But on the

other hand, have you noticed anything different about me?"

I looked at her carefully. She was the same skinny, funny Worm, eating supper in the lodge as we did every evening. "Not really."

"You see?"

"Worm, this is important. It's a little embarrassing to talk about, but I've made a lot of changes recently. Haven't you noticed any of them?" It took all my courage to say that.

"Changes like what? Don't be so mysterious."

"Well, have you noticed my legs?" I reached under the trestle table and touched my polished shins.

Worm shrugged. "Big deal. I'm probably not going to start growing hair until I'm thirty, which means I won't have to shave until I'm fifty. What else?"

"Did you notice I shaved my pits, too?" It had taken a couple of days for the bumps and nicks to heal. Then came stinging, fiery pain as I sprayed the aerosol deodorant on.

"Bets, I'm just not going to get all worked up about what you do with a razor blade. Period."

It was never hard to tell when Worm was annoyed. This must be a more sensitive area for her than I'd guessed. Worm's body had never seemed to bother her before.

"I get you, Worm, but I've got to talk to someone about this stuff. So answer me: Who are the girls that get most of the attention around here?"

She arched her eyebrows, as though unglued by the stupidity of my question. "You're asking me? When you've joined the court of one of them? Okay,

I'll bite. Bets, the ones that get the most attention are the Beauties, girls like Lolly Sharp."

"You're right, the question was a set up," I admitted. I was handling this very badly. I hadn't wanted to offend Worm, just get her to say the things I couldn't. But I had to try once more. "I know the prettiest ones are the most popular, but I still don't get it. Besides good looks, what have they got that we don't have?"

"Boyfriends," Worm said. She wadded up her napkin and left the table.

That was it.

Now that I was thinner I had to find myself a better half. Somehow I had to make myself into two, as cleanly and distinctly as the amoebas under my microscope in biology class. But there wasn't that much time left at Sunny Days. I had to work fast.

It took me a couple of days to figure it out. What might have seemed the hardest problem was really the easiest—there were no boys at camp. Oh there was Dusty, but he didn't count. At school it would have been tough indeed—first I'd have to find a boy willing to talk to me.

Finding a boyfriend at Sunny Days would be easy. It meant only a letter.

Most girls like their boyfriend. I didn't like mine at all. Actually, I'd never spoken to him. But I'd watched him, and he looked arrogant. He had a right to be, I supposed, for he was the only boy in our school who was famous. When I saw his picture in the sports page of the St. Louis newspaper, which came to me daily, a present from Mother so I wouldn't lose touch, I knew he was the one.

Duke. Two grades above me. A tennis player. The regional and state Juniors champ. A real hero. Last year he'd skipped school for three weeks to train in California, and the teachers understood perfectly. He passed everything.

And there he'd been, in the newspaper all summer, waiting for me. It was my own fault I hadn't found him sooner. Duke. He had adorable little rabbit teeth. His hair was mowed flat on top, making a square of his head. Never mind that his ears stuck out. Standing there in the newspaper picture, he displayed the biggest trophy I'd ever seen.

Victory. I snipped him and laid him in my letter box, like a pharaoh in his tomb. Duke was perfect.

Now to write the letter. I couldn't use Camp Sunny Days stationery from the canteen—obviously—nor could I use the pads of thin paper Mother had supplied for letters home—everyone had seen me write on those. Then I remembered I had packed, but ignored, a spiral notebook to practice equations for next year's hateful math class.

I belted that notebook under my robe, and left the cabin early with my flashlight, toothbrush, and pencil in my pocket. There was only one place to work privately without being discovered.

I breathed through my mouth, flashlight balanced shakily on my thigh. In the gloom of the Brown I tried to imagine what Duke's handwriting must look like. Surely it would be round and dumb. I bore down on the pencil.

My dear Betsy. Cross that out.

Hiya Betsy.

I was stumped. What on earth could he possibly

say to me? I'd have to scribble something. Anything.

Well, I'm doing real fine down here in Orlando. I trounced my opponent 6–love in the first set and stomped him 6–2 the second.

All that was safe. I'd read it in the papers. What next?

I can't write much cuz Coach says go to bed early, ha ha. So I'll send you another letter soon. I sure miss you and all those great times we had at school. I'll bet you're rooting for me every day up there with all your girlfriends. Don't forget me now.

I pondered an ending. *All my love? Goodbye darling? Sincerely?* I decided *With love, your boyfriend* was tasteful and believable, and scrawled across the paper, *Duke.*

Now came the big problem: presenting the letter. All details must be analyzed and rehearsed. When should I make my move? And where? At the mail station after lunch, or the cabin during rest hour? And how should I react to the letter I was about to receive? As I opened it, should I yell, "Help! Oh my God! Look at this!"? No, uncool. "It's about time he wrote," might be more subtle.

The risk of all this was mammoth. If I were caught—if my own handwriting was recognized through the round backhand I planned to pawn off as Duke's, then that would be it for me. Miss Mack would expose me to my parents. Worm would cry. Debbie Sue would ignore me. And this boy—Duke— would find out about it. Louise would take this little item to school and deposit it at his tennis sneakers. My disgrace would be this fall's gossip.

The first precaution was to remove all old letters from their envelopes and destroy those envelopes.

Then no one could prove Duke's letter wasn't post-marked Orlando, because I'd have no envelopes for anyone to see. I took out Mother's, double folded on heavy monogrammed stationery. I removed my father's dictated ones, typed by his secretary. Next came my grandmother's long notes about her rose garden that were like poems. The envelopes made a thick packet.

It rained the next day, chill and pelting, already hinting of fall. I eased the envelopes into my large slicker pocket and held the pocket open, encouraging big raindrops to drown them. In the Brown I took them from my pocket, their inks stained and smeared. They fluttered soggily down the dark hole, their final horrible home.

That noon, after a meager cup of soup and two saltines, I pushed along in the crowd of girls funneling through the double doors to see what news of home waited for me in my mail cubby. My grandmother's letter was wonderfully thick, just the right size for a Hershey bar. I gave it a squeeze, but it was squishy. I extracted the letter, crumpled the envelope tightly, and dumped it through the swinging trashcan lid. Then I climbed Cabin Hill to rest hour with my letter and daily newspaper. What would I learn today about Duke? Had he triumphed on the courts of Orlando? Please. I was desperate to keep him in the news a few more days. Like Debbie Sue's scrapbook, he'd prove what was real.

"Rise and shine, Bets. Shake those lazy bones. You've already missed dips!" Worm was trying to get me out of bed with her usual early morning cheer.

"I'm up, I'm up," I mumbled—but I wasn't. This was to be the day of my debut. The dawn of the new me. I couldn't move.

"Maybe we should dribble a cup of water on her," Jolee said.

"Or give her the tickle treatment!"

"It's all right, folks. Your threats are enough," I muttered from the bed. Here was everyone around me, so happy and trusting. Should I really go through with this Duke business? Maybe I didn't need to bother with this nonsense. Maybe I was just fine the way I was, without a boyfriend. But if this day was dangerous, it was also the day I'd become visible. By afternoon I'd blaze popularity like a sparkler on the Fourth of July. Didn't I have guts? Wasn't the risk worth it?

I felt fluttery as I pulled on jeans. In the muddy riding ring my horse trotted patiently while I listed again all the things that could go wrong. Maybe a better way to be noticed would be to fall off and break something serious.

I had to go to archery in my riding clothes. All my arrows wobbled, missed the target, and buried themselves in the field beyond. The class grumbled while I searched for them. When they were found, I was free to go to the cabin and change out of those smelly horse clothes.

I opened my trunk and checked the letter box, without peeking under the mustard sweater. I couldn't look at my treasures now. I must not be tempted. The clippings of Duke were in order, and the letter ready. This was my only chance. My nerve wouldn't last another day. My hand felt asleep, my arm dislocated from my body as I put the letter in my pocket.

I truly was not hungry at lunch.

In the mail room I pressed against my cubby, covering it with my stomach. I brought the Duke letter from my pocket and, as easily as if I were cheating at cards with my grandmother, slipped it under the newspaper.

The screen door announced my entrance to the cabin. Bang. I was glad for the loud noise, for I didn't trust my voice. It might be like turning on a faucet full force and getting only a drip. I'd lagged behind on the trail, giving Debbie Sue and the Cabin Fivers time to plop on their beds and begin to read mail. Now I stood in the center of the cabin, where all could see and hear. If only I could start.

"You'll never guess what I got today."

No one looked up.

I was prepared to prod them more. Or I could stop all this now. Of course they didn't care what I got today.

"Go ahead, try. You'll never guess in a million years."

"A bee sting," Worm said. I could always count on her.

"A kick in the rear from your horse," Cammy offered. She sounded nearly asleep.

I sat down on my bed and arranged a pillow self-conciously. "A letter from a boy in my class."

There was slow attention. Everyone moved their

eyes to me. My heart knocked and I knew I was flushed. There was no going back on it.

"Liar," Anna sneered. The word rested calm and sure in the cabin. No one said anything, as though she spoke for all of them.

Again it was Worm to the rescue. "Why would she lie?"

I swung the letter between my thumb and index finger, and raised my arm to show it dangling. I dared them not to believe me.

"This is true?" Wanda finally asked.

"Really?" Jolee squeaked.

I nodded solemnly to swear my truth, then let a sweeping, bashful smile of love take over my face. Oh, what an actress I was!

"Liar," Anna said again. "This has got to be a joke. How's she going to have a boyfriend? She's a liar."

"Liar my eye," I said, walking to her bed. "Watch who you're calling what, Anna Banana. Read this letter if you know how to read."

"Then why didn't you tell us before?" Cammy asked. "Why did you keep it such a big secret if it's true?"

"How did I know—maybe he wouldn't write me. There's nothing to talk about if you don't have a letter," I said smugly.

"Well, is he cute?"

"Do you go—I mean really go—with him?"

I felt their suspicions through the questions, but they believed he was real and had written me. The only one who asked me nothing was Worm. I felt rotten putting one over on Worm.

Suddenly I began to feel maybe it was all true. Now

I could say anything. Maybe Duke wasn't so made up after all. Maybe he'd secretly liked me, even loved me from afar all this time. In daydreams I'd been wooed by sultans; I'd galloped on wild ponies bare-back, pursued by warriors; I'd spent days and nights in a rowboat with the officers of my sinking ship. I had experience. I knew how love felt and it felt like this.

"Is he on a team?" Julia asked.

"On a team! He *is* the team!" I thumbed through the sports section, looking for an article on my admirer. The letter was snatched and hurled from bed to bed.

"Hey careful," I snapped. "I'm keeping that for my scrapbook."

From my letter box I took the clippings and the news photo. They double-proved there was a Duke. The Fivers were impressed. Their questions were slower now.

"Do you—like, go out on dates?" It was Anna, who'd called me a liar.

"He comes over to my house. My mother won't let me go out yet, but this year she'll give in, for sure."

They nodded.

"Well, who would have guessed."

"He sure is cute," said Debbie Sue, the last to gaze on Duke.

I smiled modestly.

But Debbie Sue was looking at me a little longer than I'd have liked. She stared down at the picture, chewing her lip, then looked at me again. Her stare told me she knew I was lying.

And now, at last, should I give it all up? Say it's all

a joke? Oh man, some people will swallow anything! I got the last laugh on you guys.

Debbie Sue handed me the photo, still looking in my eyes. "Good for you, Bets," she said. As though nothing had happened. As though she believed it all. She propped a copy of *Soap Opera Update* on her tanned legs.

Everyone began reading again. No one paid any more attention to me. I'd passed. What incredible relief. I'd done it; I won. I grinned all over inside, as satisfied—and yet as guilty—as if I'd scraped the last clinging drop of caramel sauce from a sundae cup.

10 ✳ A Frozen Heart

"**O**kay. Let me explain it to you," Lolly Sharp said. "There are two contests." She unsnapped the strap of her bathing cap and peeled it off her head.

Swimming lessons were over, the buddies counted. We'd been rehearsing for the end-of-summer Water Ballet Show; that day we'd learned to float with our legs spread, then grab our toes and sink to the weedy lake bed like a closing clam.

"The real one—the serious one—is Bathing Beauty." Lolly leaned over and dried her feet between the toes with a flowered towel. "That's the one we pay the most attention to."

Because I was late, I'd forgotten my towel. I moved out of the bath house shade into the warm sunshine to dry off. My goosebumps were severe.

"It's a pretty tense drama, really. By the time it's over almost everyone involved is crying—supposedly because they're so happy for the winner. I cried too, but I can't remember why. I think because I was so tired."

"And the other contest's the Ugly Contest, right?"

"Yup."

"So what's that like?"

Lolly started to giggle, covering both eyes with her hand, as though the memory were too much to bear. Or too embarrassing. "Oh Bets, don't make me try to explain it. You'll see for yourself."

It was that way with everyone. No one would talk about it. I began to get the idea.

Now that camp was ending, we'd entered a time of serious evaluation. Miss Mack rapped her spoon on her glass after lunch and bounced up.

"Rank tests will be given starting tomorrow morning. Your counselors want to know just what you've accomplished this summer, girls. We'll measure your progress in each activity; then we can send home reports."

Tests at camp. Tests and exams in school. Report cards here and report cards there. Would it never end? I had my Skipper Badge in sailing, my Fish in swimming, and my Captain in canoeing. I was proud of the copper necklace I'd hammered out for Mother. I'd earned no badge in riding, for though I'd finally learned to post, I was still terrified of cantering. I hadn't even thought of going off the high dive.

My main accomplishment remained secret. My treasure trove was a collection of trophies as splendid as any Duke could win. Every candy bar in my trunk was a record of will power strong as a banner headline.

Each prize represented victory over eating—something that had for so long been my sweetest comfort. Now my comfort was the collection, for it was totally private, totally mine.

My main failure seemed obvious. Though I begged my shoulders and lower back to cooperate—*hide that hump, hide that hump*—both failed me. My report would have nothing good to say about posture perfect.

Things had changed in the cabin, too. Duke wrote every few days from the Brown, and I tried hard to keep everyone interested in my love life. But Anna just shrugged now when I offered her a letter to read. I took the sports page around when there was a picture—The Fivers gave it a quick look. I had to admit, interest in Duke seemed to have faded.

Interest in almost everything seemed to have faded. There was only one consuming subject: Looks.

Rest hours I spent examining my face with a mirror secretly propped in a book. With my thumbnail I pushed at blackheads on my nose; they came out like little stones, with surprising white underbellies. I watched my forehead eruption ripen and tried to predict when it would burst.

I examined my eyebrows. Hairs had strayed down toward my eyelids. I borrowed Debbie Sue's tweezers. Clamping the pincer close to the root, I pulled hard. My flesh humped out over the eye socket before the thin hair was ripped from it. My skin flamed red.

"Try some aloe vera on it," Worm said, coming to my bed with a bottle. "It's a great skin soother. Mother wanted me to bring an entire aloe plant to camp, but she couldn't figure out how to pack it."

I hadn't realized Worm had been watching me.

Night was the best time for the Cabin Fivers to talk about Beauty. After lights out, when Debbie Sue had gone to the Counselors' Den, we settled into serious conversation. It was easier to talk in the dark; voices seemed to float without bodies from the beds.

"I don't see what's wrong with coloring your hair. A little frosting just helps highlight it, that's all," Jolee said.

"Dye dries out your hair—didn't you know that? In a few years you'll have scalp to shoulder split ends." It was Wanda's voice.

"It depends on what kind you use. My mom uses Cellophane—it lets the natural beauty of your hair shine through," Cammy chimed in from her corner.

"It's not natural to use dye," Worm said.

"Come off it, Worm. You'd probably dye your hair with carrot juice."

"That shows how little you know about natural products, Cammy. There's henna, which has been around for centuries."

"I would never use anything that old on *my* hair!"

"And of course there's lemon juice. That does the same thing as frosting," Worm continued.

I knew Jolee wouldn't like that. She was mighty proud of her white-flecked hair. And I needed to have a little talk with Worm about not pushing all this health business on the cabin. A lot of the Fivers thought it was pretty strange.

"There are other things you can do to your hair besides put chemicals on it. You could use beer rinses," Worm said defiantly.

"And get kicked out of camp."

"Or you could rinse it in salt water every half hour and sit in the sun."

I longed for blonde hair. Debbie Sue had said she'd buy dye on her day off for anyone who wanted it, but I dared not try life as a blonde. I knew Mother was going to be so happy to see me thinner, and hair even a teeny bit blonde might ruin it all.

When we left our hair and talked about our bodies, it made me nervous. Besides the issue of fat, I'd noticed several secret things I didn't want discovered. There were little white bumps on my arms I'd rather not think about. I was afraid pubic hair had started creeping down my thighs. My navel was too big. But as long as we talked about the perfect body—in the dark—it was safe.

"So what's it take to make a perfect Beauty Queen?" Dawn asked.

"For openers, her face has to be a classic oval," Wanda said.

I remembered learning to write script in third grade, tracing ovals until my hand ached. I'd never make my face look like that.

"And she's got to have big boobs. But not droopy, you know?"

"What makes tits sag anyway?"

"Beats me. Ask Miss Mack, she's had experience."

I hawked a loud laugh that sounded like a snore.

"You know what I heard about Miss Mack?" Dede said.

"That she's a hundred and two."

"No really. I heard she'd once been a Beauty Queen. She won some big contest."

How I'd have loved to tell them about those weird old photographs on her wall—but I'd promised Lolly.

"Go on. When she was young there weren't even contests yet."

"Let's get back to *real* Bathing Beauties. Do you think anyone with a waistline over twenty-four inches stands a chance?" Dawn asked.

Of course I couldn't measure up to that. I'd never get my waist thin enough. No one could fill the ideal Beauty in every way, but I didn't think, all things considered, I was so bad—no worse than lots of campers, examined section by section. One thing was sure: I wasn't a candidate for the Ugly Contest.

Who was?

Anna Banana was in the bed next to mine. She'd been homesick all summer and spent most rest hours writing her parents long letters. Her teeth were bucked, though I only noticed this when she smiled. Anna kept a bottle of allergy pills on her trunk top, along with petrified wads of Kleenex. Her face was often blotched red. She was definitely a candidate.

And though I hated to admit it, so was Worm. No matter how often she washed it, her hair was stringy and dripped in gluey clumps. Purple pimples marked the places it brushed her back and shoulders. At the bottom of her skinny body she had big calves, with muscles knotted high on her legs, almost behind her knees. I mainly liked to think about her eyes— amazing emeralds ringed with fur. And she tanned to polished bronze. But I knew her health-nut ideas didn't sit well with most people, and I was afraid most of the Fivers would consider her bad points more than her good. Yes, she was our other possibility for Bathing Ugly.

There were candidates to represent our cabin in the Beauty Contest, too—obvious ones. I studied them, trying to imagine how it would feel. In my heart of hearts I knew it was most unlikely I'd be chosen. This made me feel both sad and safe. I wouldn't have to parade around in my bathing suit in front of Dusty or Miss Mack. That meant I wouldn't get any applause, but I wouldn't get stares either. Ah, but if I were beautiful, maybe I'd want stares. How could I know?

As it became late, talk of Beauty slowed. My eyes were too heavy to open. Beauty drifted in front, sparkling and magic like the good witch of Oz.

There was a buzz, whispers.

"Hey Bets."

Something poked my feet. I was instantly awake. I understood completely and immediately what was happening.

In the dark I groped for my bathrobe. "If you'd only lay your clothes out neatly the night before," Mother would say, "you could find them." I heard a blanket being ripped from a bed and did the same—wrapped it Indian style over my pajamas. A round spot of light danced on the floor.

"Get your flashlights. Let's go." It was a growly hiss, loud enough for all to hear.

Go where? I knew enough to keep my flashlight low, so the counselor on patrol wouldn't check us. I pressed the end into my palm and switched it on, making my hand glow eerily.

Someone was in charge, but I wasn't sure who. The light spot drew a circle on the floor, tracing it several times. That was our meeting place, the clearing between the beds. I walked to it blindly, ramming my leg into a bed frame.

"Well," our leader began—halted—then took a deep breath. "We all know what we're here for. Turn off your flashlights."

I relaxed. That voice of authority was only Cammy. Of course she was our leader—she'd been in the Beauty Contest last year so she couldn't be in it this year. That was the rule. Now she could tell us what to do.

"Is everyone here?"

Cammy shined her light around the circle, lingering on each face. Our eyes squinched up from the glare. Everyone looked tense and determined. I watched the light travel, dreading the moment it would pin me like an insect to a mounting board.

"Okay. For the new girls, here's how we do it." Cammy flicked off the flashlight. We were in blackest darkness separated from each other by an inky ocean, with only Cammy's voice to guide us. "We're going to choose a Bathing Beauty and a Bathing Ugly tonight. To make this fair, we'll give everyone a chance at both."

Sounded fair all right. But who wanted a chance at Ugly?

"We'll go around the circle one at a time. When it's your turn, tell what you think your best feature is, for Beauty, and your worst, for Ugly."

That should be simple. The instructions were clear: best and worst. We were all quiet. My brain churned for an idea, a way to change what was going to happen. I felt panicked. I couldn't think of one good feature. No one else was worried—just like the weigh-ins. They were quietly sorting good, better, best points.

I raked over my face. My strawberry nose? Why did Mother call it that, anyway? Because of my blackheads? My ears? Mother said they were flat, perfect little seashells, but that didn't count for much. The back of my neck? Daddy called it "neckus" and gave me kisses on the base of my skull. Surely that couldn't be my best feature.

Cammy was beginning. I could only worry about myself with half attention since I had to hear what everyone else said.

"Dede."

Dede was silent.

Cammy hissed her name again.

"My nose," Dede blurted. The flashlight wavered on her nose.

Nice enough, I thought, but not special. A little too flat on the end.

"Okay Dede. Now your worst feature." It was a command. The light was still on her face.

"My ankles," she whispered.

Why? There was nothing wrong with her ankles.

Dede's rigid face was left to darkness as the flashlight played at the hem of her blanket. It searched for her ankles to expose the worst. Hopeless. Her feet were tucked under the cover, her shame hidden. I realized that's why she'd chosen her ankles. Ha!

The one thing they couldn't check on. Before I could define Dede's real worst feature, the flashlight had gone on to the next camper.

We all stared at Dawn. "Dawn, what's your best feature?"

"I don't know. But I know for sure what my worst is."

What? She had tons of good features.

"My teeth mess up the whole way I look. They're so crooked. They've got spaces between them and there's one that's a big fang. I hate having people look at my mouth." Dawn's words chased each other without breath.

The flashlight shone steadily on her mouth, her straight, unsmiling lips pressed over her teeth. I'd never thought they were bad. It was Anna who was bucked. Perhaps I'd never really seen Dawn's.

As though we'd all thought that at once, the voice of Cammy from the dark commanded, "Show us your teeth, Dawn."

"No." Her lips made a little circle in the middle, revealing nothing. "I've told but I'm not going to show."

"Come on Dawn, that's not fair. You've got to," a voice whined. The flashlight hung on her mouth in the quiet. The Fivers waited.

When she drew back her lips, they pulled up dangerously over wet, pink gums. I was dazzled by the teeth—crooked, menacing as a frightened horse. Ready to bite. Then her lips snapped back into place, her head went straight. It was Dawn again. I wasn't sure what I'd seen, it was all too fast.

"Have you tried brushing with peroxide and baking soda? There's a lot of harmful sugar in toothpaste, you know."

"Shut up Worm," someone said.

"Anna. Your best. Your worst."

The flashlight prodded out answers, one at a time around the circle. Several times I became confused and forgot whether we were on best or worst.

"My father's chin."

"I have a short neck."

"The birthmark on my lip. It looks like a mustache."

No one'd mentioned fat pads or saddlebags or double chins. The closer the flashlight came to me, the calmer I felt. No way they'd find out what I really thought. I'd lied about Duke and I could lie again. I wouldn't tell them my best feature was my stomach now that it was flat. I wouldn't say my worst was my rear which still bulged. Best, worst: When you lie it's all the same.

"Betsy."

It was my turn to squint into the beam. I was surprised to find, now that I knew what I was going to do, that I liked the attention. I tried to look modest.

"I've always liked my dimples."

I didn't, but Mother's friends would tell me how charming they were. When they asked for a big smile, I stretched my mouth wide and sucked in my cheeks.

"Your worst."

"My forehead."

Surprise—a half truth. Since I first grew hair I'd worn bangs to cover a too-long forehead. Every week Mother trimmed them, protecting my eyes with Kleenex. Now, underneath bangs, my forehead sprouted pimples like weeds in a moist, shady place.

The flashlight moved on. It had worked, they'd passed me. No questions about the truth. No one said, "What about your butt, you didn't mention that." No one called me on a flabby upper arm. The flashlight simply went on.

"My widow's peak."

"My knees. Mom tells me not to lock them when I stand, but I forget. I just can't help it." It was Worm.

"My chewed-up fingernails."

"My bony feet. They look like claws."

"I have a big appendix scar. I'll never be able to wear a bikini."

"Have you tried vitamin E? They say it makes scars disappear."

"Shut up Worm. This isn't the time for your quack ideas." Our leader was mad.

We'd finished the circle, except for Cammy. Smugly she said, "I don't have to tell because I can't be in the contest anyway. And now," she announced, "it's time to vote. I've got pencils and paper. This is a secret ballot, so keep your flashlights low and don't let anyone see what you've written. Fold your paper good and tight when you're finished."

She demonstrated, pressing a paper into a small package of folds. Of course we'd always done this when we passed notes in school. There was nothing to learn from Cammy, but we let her show us how anyway. She was in charge of this choosing.

I was nudged by a pad of paper being passed from my right. Pencils rolled around on top. I slid one off and tore a sheet from the pad. There was no noise but the sound of the papers' progress around the circle. The floor was icy. I sat cross-legged, my toes poking out into the cold. My ankles ground into the boards. I hunched into my blanket.

"Okay girls, let's get this straight." Cammy sounded like a counselor or a teacher, not like one of the Fivers. "We've had a chance to see the best and worst of everybody."

Not me. I wouldn't let them know my worst, and my best wasn't ready to be shown yet.

"The honor of Cabin Five is at stake." Cammy raised her voice above the whisper our midnight mission required. "It's a team effort. We've got to have top-notch contestants to win. Let's bring home those prizes."

That sack of candy bars. If I couldn't have the triumph of walking in with it, of being the one who handed them out, at least I could vote responsibly. I could make sure one of our girls won.

But here was the terrible dilemma. I knew I shouldn't let personality get in the way—I shouldn't think about who I liked best or least. I should vote straight for the ugliest and the prettiest. But I knew Ugly was going to be Worm. Not only was she borderline on looks, but I could tell the cabin was really annoyed with her. And Worm was someone I wanted as a good friend forever. If the ballot was unanimous for her, she was going to be very hurt. She was going to get nominated all right, but I really didn't want to be a part of it.

I wrote the names, holding my light and dutifully

shielding the paper as though it were a Latin exam. I chose Wanda for Beauty. I'd known that all summer—there wasn't much to decide. For Ugly, I wrote in my own name.

While Cammy walked the inside of the circle with a box, collecting ballots, I shivered nervously. I couldn't stand to see Worm clobbered. More than anything, I hoped she wouldn't cry. But I planned to help her—after all, she'd have to understand it was all in fun. Nobody took it seriously.

Cammy sat on the bed with the cigar box, her back to us. We knew she was unfolding little squares, flattening out the creases with her fingers. I remembered when Wanda had been crowned Miss Posture Perfect of the Week, at the council fire. She accepted the honor without surprise, as though it were her right.

Cammy's voice came from far away, tunneled through her back. "I'm adding up the totals now."

It took a long time. I wiggled my cold toes, though that made them ache more. I stared into the darkness.

"Attention everyone." Cammy's voice swung around loudly in the cabin.

The group was silent. There was no question of attention.

"We have two clear-cut winners. No doubt about it, this year we'll bring home two prizes for Cabin Five."

I was ready for it. I'd be the first to congratulate Worm. I'd make her feel good about it somehow.

"Wanda Suzicki is Bathing Beauty."

"Hurray!"

"Way to go, Wanda!"

"And Betsy Sherman is Bathing Ugly."

"Hot dog, Bets." I was punched on the arm.

"Atta gal, you'll be great."

"You can do it, Bets. You can win." It was Worm's voice.

My cabinmates couldn't see me. At least they couldn't see the hot color of my face, or my hands pinching each other. As though I was in a great cave, I heard congratulations bouncing all over, echoing.

I couldn't see Wanda. I imagined her smiling in the dark, turning her head serenely. I could do that too.

"Thank you," I said. It sounded stony. I tried again. "Thanks everyone."

The Fivers got up, hitched their blankets around their shoulders and went to their beds. I uncrossed my legs and eased up on stiff knees. I tested my ankles. My heart had frozen; each muscle of my face had crystallized and set. Well, look what's happened to me, I thought. At least my feet aren't cold anymore.

11 * Talking Ugly

So that was it. It didn't matter if I got thin or not. I was Bathing Ugly. That was one question I wouldn't have to ask Mother—now I had the absolute answer, underlined. Thin was not the secret to solving all my problems.

As Worm and I walked to breakfast the morning after the choosing, I could see all the cabins had done the same thing the night before. It was easy to pick out the Beauties. They sauntered down the trail with straight backs and swaggering hips.

I could pick out the Uglies too. They looked the way I felt—bewildered and very much alone. What if I walked next to one and said: "Don't take it so hard. It's all a joke—it's got to be. And look! Cheer up, because I'm here too. Last night they picked me to be an Ugly and, well, you know what I mean. I may not be ready for the Beauty Contest, but come on, I'm not exactly Ugly."

"Oh yes you are, Betsy-babes," the Ugly would say,

"and the sooner you get that idea through your thick head the better off you'll be. Say it. Ugly. Ugly."

We climbed over benches and sat at the trestle table. Worm had been unusually quiet this morning. I wondered if somehow she suspected I'd voted for myself to spare her the humiliation of a unanimous choice. Well, that certainly had backfired. Not that it mattered—I could still hear Cammy's words, "We have two clear-cut winners." That meant it wasn't even close.

Worm took a round plastic box from her pocket and put it between us on the table. As she opened it, the smell made me a baby again, with a spoon of dark, thick liquid coming straight toward me. "Have a vitamin," Worm said. "It'll do you a world of good."

"No thanks. Somehow that doesn't seem to be what I need."

"Give it a try. When my mom's nerves are bad, she always doubles her B-vitamins. They're good for coping with stress."

"There's nothing wrong with my nerve."

"Not your nerve, your nerves. There's a difference, you know."

"Look, I know what I need, Worm," I said, looking down at my mushy white cereal. "I need you to pass the sugar."

"Oh well, it's your body. And not a bad one at that, if you ask me."

I hesitated for a second, then tossed on a spoonful so heaping it rained down on the way from the sugar bowl. What difference did it make what I ate? I slurped my cereal as fast as I could. Then I helped

myself to three pieces of bacon, sandwiched them
between jellied toast, and mashed it all together. The
crunch, the crumbs, the sweetness of it. I dropped a
marshmallow in my cocoa. It bobbed on top, shining
and spreading as it melted.

Full at last. But not full of pleasure.

Miss Mack's spoon clanked her glass for attention.
"Good morning, girls. It's a lovely morning, a posture
perfect morning."

Campers jerked up taller on their benches. Two
tables away, I saw Louise click into ramrod position.
I collapsed down so far my back looked more like a
camel than a human.

"I'm sure we'll see lots of straight backs today, as
we prepare for that most glorious of all Sunny Days
traditions, the Bathing Beauty Contest."

I squinched up my face hard until I knew I had
Miss Mack's expression.

"And tomorrow we will see at long last who is
fairest of them all in our little kingdom!" Miss Mack
pulled herself to the toes of her high-tops, bouncing
like a dribbled basketball.

My mouth puckered and I made my eyes bulge. I
turned my face to Worm and tapped her arm. She
tried not to laugh, but holding it made her choke on
her cereal. When she showered her mouthful back
into her bowl, milk leaking from her nose, I knew
I'd been a success, of sorts.

After breakfast I headed for the arts and crafts
barn. I needed a dark, protected place. At home I
used to take a blanket into the back yard, and safe
under the big sycamore tree I'd spread it on the

grass. Then I'd lie at one end and roll myself up in it like an apple strudel, and the bad would go away.

I let my eyes adjust to the dark inside the barn door. Most Sunny Days campers used these last hours to earn more badges. "Don't waste your time indoors, girls," Miss Mack said over and over. "Every moment spent outside is precious." But for me there was only one, huge challenge ahead.

I immediately noticed two Uglies from other cabins as I entered. So I not only looked like an Ugly, I was behaving like one, too, hiding away in here. I stood in front of the shelves that held the Wishing Boats each camper had been required to make. We'd whittled small blocks of balsa into hulls, and drilled mast holes. I stared at the little boats lying on their sides as though they'd been shipwrecked.

"Haven't finished yours either?"

I whirled around. I hadn't seen Lolly Sharp come in. Last year's Beauty.

"Not yet." Lie: I had. Started and finished it in an hour, when I'd learned about the wishing boats.

"The final moment of camp, girls," Miss Mack had said, "you'll write your deepest wish and make the paper into a sail for your Wishing Boat. The evening breeze will carry them off to the Land Where All Wishes Are Granted."

"I haven't finished mine because I think that's a lot of bull about wishes coming true," Lolly said. "Except it's not—since everyone is supposed to wish they'll come back to Sunny Days next year, and somehow everyone does."

I laughed. My voice sounded strange, as though it needed oiling.

Lolly took a piece of sandpaper and found her boat. "Hey, I hear you'll be in the contest."

Now there was one way of putting it: I'll be in the contest. Not an Ugly, just in the contest.

"That's good, Bets. You'll be the perfect one to do it."

My face drained, leaving just the tingle at the side of my nose that meant tears. It got larger. The perfect one. I looked back over my shoulder as though I'd heard someone coming behind me. That was stalling, I knew. I mustn't cry in front of Lolly, of all people. How could she have said that? Lolly was the one who'd said I was terrific at the time I most needed to hear it. And I'd believed her.

"Hey Bets, you're too quiet. Say something. Listen, don't misunderstand me."

No indeed.

"I mean some girls get so upset by it all."

Yes.

"They take it seriously, they forget it's a joke—a weird joke. It's supposed to be funny, Bets—but most of the Uglies get it wrong."

Wrong? I stayed twisted, looking back over my shoulder.

"They think they're Ugly because of that stupid Beauty Contest. They're not, of course."

Oh come off it, I thought. How could this Beauty stand there and say this gibberish?

"They just have to dress Ugly for the contest, you see. Pretend Ugly that day."

Oh man, was that how they billed it? I wasn't taken in. Everyone knew Bathing Beauties look wonderful all the time, not for just one day. Now Lolly wanted me to believe that Bathing Uglies look just as good, but make themselves ugly for the fun of it?

I turned back to Lolly. "So you're trying to tell me that the contest for Beauty is serious, for real. Miss Mack will crown the fairest of them all. Then the Uglies will parade on for a moment of make believe?"

"That's it, you got it." But she looked doubtful, as though she'd listened to herself for the first time. We were quiet for a few moments. "I guess you're right," she said at last. "I don't really know what the contest means. But I know one thing, you're strong enough to do it. You won't crumple." She put her slender arm around my shoulder.

Maybe that was right. Better me than Worm—her eyes would be red and swollen this morning if she'd been elected Ugly. Thinking of Worm made the prickling under my lip begin to subside.

"I'll tell you, Bets, I've got a feeling you're going to show them all how to do it. I think maybe you'll just teach them a thing or two."

Maybe I'd do that. Maybe I would.

Lolly bent over her sanding, as controlled and graceful as a ballet dancer. "It's all about as stupid as these Wishing Boats, if you ask me."

"How can you use a word like stupid when you've been Beauty?"

"Because being Beauty is nothing, that's why. It's like sanding this dumb boat. It just grinds you down."

"Poop. That's easy to say when you're gorgeous."

"Gorgeous? What does that mean?" She raised shining hazel eyes to me. "You've seen Miss Mack's pictures. You've heard the rumors. Even Miss Mack was gorgeous once. Where does it get you in the long run?"

"Well, I wouldn't mind giving good looks a try."

"You think so now, but then everyone makes such a big deal out of your looks—and that's not something you can even help."

I thought of my fat lost ounce by painful ounce. My legs and armpits scraped clean. The hair yanked from my eyebrows. I was trying hard for help.

"If you only knew, Bets. Most of the time I walk around feeling like a complete fake."

Lolly Sharp? A fake riding around inside that magic bubble?

"I can't explain it. It's like being pretty makes me into a phony sometimes. I have to pretend a lot. I mean I have to be who other kids want me to be, not who I feel like. It seems like I'm always practicing, and I don't know what it's for." She shook her head sadly; little ringlets wisped around her face, golden in the window light. "It sounds stupid, but it's not all laughs, I promise you."

Was Lolly looking for pity? If so she wouldn't get it here. If we could just switch places for a few weeks, if I could only try that phony life of hers for a little while, then maybe I'd work up a tear.

"So what are you going to wish for?" I asked, looking at the smooth hull of Lolly's little boat.

"Same old thing. What I'm expected to." Lolly lowered her eyes, long lashes brushing her cheek. "I

wish I can be a Sunny Days camper again next year."
She opened them. "There. What about you?"

"I'm not telling." In truth, I didn't know. There
were all the things I'd wished for before, but they
seemed to have gotten me nowhere. Mother had
begun this wishing-wanting business, and I'd gone
along with it, wishing I could be a Beauty. Now—
though I wouldn't tell Lolly—it seemed the only wish
left was to be alone with my treasure chest.

"I bet I know! You're wishing you'll win that
contest!"

Wishing I could fall straight through to China
rather than have to parade in front of Miss Mack
and Dusty. Wishing Lolly would take her tiny waist
and big mouth out of here. Wishing this day would
end, and the next one, and the day after that. Wishing
it were time for lunch.

New temptations. At breakfast I'd given in to greed
and misery as savagely as a starving dog with a garbage
can. Now again, there were choices. When the dish
of macaroni and cheese was passed, would I neatly
serve out a taste or shake huge globs off the spoon?
Bread? How much? Butter? How about apple crisp?
With whipped cream?

I gave in. Wolfed it down. I was stuffed for the
first time in eight weeks. But instead of spreading
through me, making me feel good all over, the food
seemed to lump in my stomach. I tried to remember
the old, pre-diet satisfaction of fullness, but it was no
good. I knew something I didn't want to admit: Being

full was no longer going to make everything all right, any more than being empty had.

As I walked up Cabin Hill to rest hour, I saw that plate of macaroni again, saw it mounded yellow like little rubber hoses stuck together in glue sauce. I'd never liked it, and I'd taken three helpings. Why, why, oh why? Now there was no chance for my diet—I'd blown it completely. No point wishing to be thin. My skin fit tight again.

I told myself it didn't matter. The weigh-ins were over. The choosing was over. Last night, sitting in that dark circle I realized no one had any real idea what they looked like. Everyone saw something different in themselves from what others saw. So why should any of it matter?

My treasure trove. Maybe I could be the first one back to the cabin. I could check on my wealth. Maybe I could even sample a corner of a Peanut Crunch. I hurried.

Everyone was there.

Magazines—*Vogue, Seventeen, Redbook*—were strewn on Debbie Sue's bed, their spines cracked open to hairstyles. Magic markers circled make-up tricks.

"Look at this one," Dede called as I came in the door. "Of course she's such a doll anything would look great on her."

Wanda was perched on the end of Debbie Sue's bed, head arched high as a queen already. Debbie Sue stood above her, spritzing on setting lotion and smoothing it through her hair. Dede was her hand-maiden, handing up fat pink rollers.

"We're trying out this one." Debbie Sue nodded at

a propped magazine. She pulled a section of hair around the curler and tightly rolled it under. Wanda shifted a quarter turn. Debbie Sue wet the next section and sticky lotion trickled down Wanda's neck.

"There, at last," Debbie Sue sighed.

Wanda sat posture perfect, a feast of plump sausages crowning her head. Debbie snared the front curlers in a sleazy blue net, pulled it firmly over the rest, and tied the ends in a double knot.

"If only we had electricity in this place I could have blown you dry," Debbie Sue grumbled. "Wouldn't have had to bother with all this. But you'll have to sit in the sun to dry it now."

Wanda left obediently for the steps. I realized there must be fifteen other Sunny Days Beauties dotting the steps of Cabin Hill, each in her own sunlight.

"Okay kiddos. Swimsuits." Debbie Sue was matter-of-fact. "Everyone get out their swimsuits. Put them on this bed."

"Why? Mine's still wet," Anna said.

"Because, Miss Anna Banana, we've got to pick the best suit for our Beauty."

Mine was still damp, too, and was pinned by the crotch to the clothesline outside.

Debbie spread them gently on the bed, arranging their collapsed shapes as though they were waiting for bodies. Only the ones with foam cups looked alive, jutting up on the bed. Most were skinny, shriveled tank suits, with high-cut legs and string straps.

"Someday Miss Mack's going to get with it and let us wear bikinis here," Julia said.

My bathing suit was seersucker, the only one with a skirt. I hated it. Mother had said a skirt does wonders for dimply back thighs.

"Let's see," Debbie Sue mused. "We've got to consider size, color, and style." Her eyes circled the bed, taking close inventory. "Bets, you'll be needing yours for Ugly, so why don't you take it now." She didn't look up. "Hmmm, blue. That's a good color for Wanda. Let's pick a couple, then get her in here to try them on."

I tramped outside to the drying line with my damp suit. There was no point being angry—after all, someone had to be Ugly. Wanda was drooped on the steps, fist holding her cheek. Sweat beaded her pink forehead.

"These curlers make my head feel miserable. I'm so hot I could melt," she said. She looked at me as though I might rescue her, trade places somehow.

"Anything for Beauty," I said, flouncing by.

In the cabin Dawn and Jolee knelt on the floor over a wide red satin ribbon. They had a tape measure, pencils, glue, and a bucket of fine white sand. They sketched big letters on the ribbon, *Wanda, Cabin Five*. Her name and our cabin number would run between her breasts from hip to shoulder, identifying her like a breakfast cereal at the supermarket. Absurd, I thought. By the end of camp everyone knew Wanda's name and cabin number. She didn't need that thing.

I sat on my bed watching Jolee spread the Elmer's carefully, then drizzle sand over the glue letters. I thought of my own letters lying in my treasure trunk.

Oh, how Duke had let me down. He didn't make me a Beauty. He was the Duke of nothing. The Duke of disappointment. The respect he brought me was so fleeting it was hardly worth my effort. I thought if Duke loved me it would make everyone else love me. Popularity created more popularity. It seemed to work for a little while, but there'd been less excitement every day.

"Your boyfriend hasn't done much for your backhand," Cammy complained when she was my tennis partner the week before. Was she putting down me or Duke? He really hadn't lived up to his responsibilities. I'd expected too much. And he didn't even write interesting letters.

There was a sadder and deeper truth, too. The only thing I'd really gained from Duke was a title: The Duchess of Lies.

Wanda had been released from the sun and was trying on suits. She stepped into them easily and wiggled them up her body. They all looked marvelous.

"I'm not sure blue really is the best color for her eyes," Debbie Sue said.

Green, yellow, stripes, patterns—they all were fine.

"I don't know what we can do about this fanny overhang of yours," Debbie Sue said, tugging critically at the bottom of a pink suit. "Try on another one."

"Well," Debbie Sue said doubtfully, "while the blue one is cut higher and makes your legs look longer, you could use some shaping up top, don't you agree girls?"

If Wanda could use shaping, what could I use?

"One of these three," Debbie Sue announced. "Absolutely. We'll make our final decision later. Now chickadees, here's our next job." She slid a cardboard box from under her bed and unflapped its top. It was filled with shoes.

"We got first crack at them! I beat the other counselors to the dramatics closet." She dumped them out.

"Hey look, there are some gold platforms with ankle straps!"

"I'd take those satin spike heels. I adore pastels."

"Can you believe it? Those mules have ostrich feathers."

Julia squatted on the floor acting like Prince Charming with the glass slipper, while Wanda tried on every pair. Some flopped, some squeezed, pinched, bulged up her arch. Some fit. Wanda strutted the cabin length without wobbling. The Fivers tossed the discarded shoes back in the box.

What about me? I thought. I gazed at the shoes like they were a movie gone out of focus. What about me? I was supposed to be in the contest too. No one had said a thing about Bathing Ugly. Wrong. Debbie Sue had told me to wear my own bathing suit. Did Uglies get high heels? I didn't know the rules. I did know, however, that this box would soon be going back to dramatics. If I was to have shoes, it must be now. Focus returned.

I scooted next to Debbie Sue. This must all be done quietly, without the fanfare of Beauty.

"Is it okay for me to take shoes?" I whispered. "You know, something funny? For the contest?"

"Sure. Take anything you want." Debbie Sue was pulling items from her zippered make-up kit, arranging them on a plastic tray. Absorbed, she uncapped a lipstick, checked the color, rolled it down. Dawn and Jolee were finishing the Beauty ribbon. Cammy checked through the fashion magazines. Anna, Dede, and Julia tried swatches of eyeshadow— sea green, dust gray, soft blue—on the backs of their hands. Worm read a magazine alone.

I rummaged through the shoe box. I knew exactly the pair I wanted. They weren't funny at all. Silver leather sandals with heels that tapered to a pencil width, straps that wove across the instep and had tiny gold buckles. They'd dangled on Wanda's feet when she tried them—though she pulled the straps as tight as possible.

They fit me. I knew they would. Quickly I had them on and off. I eased them under my pillow. Later I'd slip them in my trunk, snuggle them against my candy treasure. Tomorrow in the contest I'd wear my Ugly clothes, but the silver shoes too.

"How thin her ankles are," everyone would say. "She should wear those shoes more often."

"Well, I have a pair just like them at home," I'd say. "I wear them out with Duke."

Debbie Sue unlocked curlers from Wanda's head and tossed them on the bed. Wanda's hair twisted down in odd corkscrews of stuck-together clumps. Debbie Sue combed and patted. She pulled her hair straight up, sprayed it with mousse, then combed it the wrong way, to make it stand alone like a barberry hedge. She smoothed and pushed hair over the snarls.

"Uh-uh. All wrong. Your forehead's much too high." Wanda's face sagged. "I mean, it looks like a wig on you." She took apart the teasing with her fingers, pulling out tangles above Wanda's winced forehead. "I don't know what we'll do now. I guess cutting it's the only possibility."

I surveyed the make-up tray—tubes, jars, pencils, little brushes. Were those the things I would need tomorrow? What, exactly, was I doing tomorrow? I was sure of one thing: Whatever it was, it was up to me. Directions wouldn't be given to Uglies. Debbie Sue wouldn't fix my hair or stroke mascara on my lashes. The Fivers wouldn't choose my clothes. No ribbon was being made to go across my chest. Whatever I did was going to be my own.

12 ✳ A Little Tea Party

"Panty raid, panty raid, panty raid!" Flashlights jiggled around the cabin like motorcycle headlights. Something metal dropped on the floor.

I woke up fast.

"All right you dumb Fivers, this is it." The voice came from the center of the room, creaky and horse. The beam from its light swung around. "Prepare yourselves, creeps!"

Someone was in the cabin, with a cloudy voice and a light beam for an eye. And there were others.

"What's going on?" It was Cammy—not the Cammy who had led us so confidently through the choosing, but a new one, scared, her voice quavering.

"Where's Debbie Sue?" Worm called out unsteadily.

I sat up in bed jolted by fear. Cammy didn't know what was going on—this was nothing planned. This was no part of the contest. And Debbie Sue must be in the Counselors' Den. Without Debbie Sue there was no one to help us. We were in trouble.

Flashlights flicked; strange rhythmic thumps came from the floor. They were doing some sort of war dance, loud and invisible. This was an attack.

"Come on guys, what do you want here?" Anna's whine was stronger than Cammy's voice.

"Come on guys, come on guys," the creaky voice mimicked.

"Hey let's quit wasting time!" It was one of *them*. "Patrol counselor will be around soon. Let's get to it."

"So you want to know who we are?" another snarled from the doorway. "Too bad, kiddies, it ain't that easy."

"Go on, tell 'em. They'll find out anyway." The invader drummed her feet in the dance again, light jerking around. "Tell 'em."

"We're the Caw Caw Taws, that's who!"

The what? My fear relaxed. Caw Caw? What kind of name was that? It sounded like the noise blue jays make.

"That's us, kiddies. You've heard of the Kappa Kappa Gammas and the Sigma Delta Nus—and now you know the Caw Caw Taws."

"So what do you want from us?" Cammy's voice sounded back in control now.

"Your underwear's going to be at the top of that flagpole tomorrow morning, that's what. Your farewell present to Miss Mack, idiot child."

"Oh come on, that's ridiculous," Julia called out. "What a stupid, unoriginal thing to do."

Exactly what I was thinking.

Julia's bed was surrounded by lights. Feet pounded the floor like charging elephants. "That's what you think, do ya girlie? Well, we'd better make sure your undies are the first ones up there."

I heard things on top of Julia's trunk crash to the floor. They were going through Julia's trunk!

"Hey stop that, I'm going to report you." Julia'd found her flashlight and now she shined it hard onto an intruder's face.

I saw a pale head, all of flesh, eyes drawn out, nose flattened. It was a monster's face with no cheeks, and the lower half was round, with thick fish lips.

"Oh my God."

"Yuck. What's wrong with her?"

"Don't be scared, there's nothing wrong." I distinctly heard my own voice speaking calmly. "That's just a stocking she's wearing over her head. She thinks it's still Halloween."

"Whoa there." The light left Julia's bed and the top of her trunk slammed down. "I think we've got a new little problem over in this corner of the room."

Lights wavered toward me. I knew I was in for it. "Hey wait a minute. I didn't mean anything. Can't you take a joke?"

The lights advanced. Fright became panic—I wanted to race screaming from my bed. Lights were menacing toward me, four or five of them, almost on top of me.

"Well, well, well. Who have we here? Look what the scouting party has uncovered. If it isn't little Betsy-babes. Oh pardon me, forget the little. It's good old, big old Betsy-babes."

The croaking voice disguised nothing. It was Louise.

"Yeah, it's me. So what?" I knew I had to back off,

say nothing to provoke her. But I couldn't help the words that bubbled out, for they beat back dread like water on a burning house.

"I think this is the young lady we've come to visit." Louise sat on my bed. I felt others sit around my legs, imprisoning them under my blanket. "In fact, I think this is why we made this late-night trip in the first place, don't you girls?"

"Maybe. It might just be."

"I do believe we've come to the right place."

"Come off it, Louise. I know who you are—you've never been too great an actress." My panic mixed with anger. What right had Louise to invade my cabin in the middle of the night with these goons?

"I think we should talk about it. I think we should sit down right here and have a little chat. After all, no one's going anyplace soon." Louise shined the light at the doorway. "Everything still clear outside?"

"Not a creature is stirring."

"Good. Now let's get this straight, Betsy-babes. I am not Louise. I'm going to do you a great favor and tell you my top secret Caw Caw Taw name, and from now on when you address me, use it."

"I don't care what you call yourself, Louise."

"Panther. That's the name and you better get used to it quick. Say it—Panther."

No one in the cabin spoke. No one coughed. No one laughed.

"And now let's have our little tea party. Are you pouring, Betsy-babes?" Louise's voice was sugary.

"I don't know what you're talking about, Louise."

"Uh-uh. The name's Panther. Let's not forget

again. So, no tea tonight. Too bad. I guess you weren't expecting us."

"No, not exactly, so maybe you'd better go now."

"Oh well then, on to other things. Hmmm, I wonder how a pair of your big old grimy underpants would look hooked up on the pole instead of Old Glory?"

"Louise—I mean Panther—that's just so juvenile I can't believe you're saying it." I knew my goal was to keep her out of my trunk. And I remembered it when I called her "Panther," but my anger was in control by the time I got to "juvenile." By the end of the sentence, I knew I was in big trouble.

"Oh yes, that's Panther's problem. She's such a juvenile. And Betsy-babes is all grown up, a regular adult. Why she even shaves her legs. Haven't you seen her, girls?"

The Caw Caw Taws grunted.

"Fivers, haven't you seen her shave?"

The cabin was silent.

"Never mind. I guess everyone's a little tongue tied. Back to being a grown-up. It takes more than shaved legs to be a grown-up, doesn't it girls? And I hear our Betsy-babes has something all the big girls have. What could that be?"

"It's sure not big boobs," a Caw Caw Taw snorted.

"Let me tell you—and please correct me if I'm wrong—Betsy-babes has a boyfriend."

Oh God. Duke. Oh no.

"What's his name?" Louise demanded.

I clenched my hands to fists.

"I say out there, who can tell me his name?"

The Fivers had learned from my big mouth. The

Caw Caw Taws were on my bed, not theirs. They remained silent.

"No takers, huh? Well, I understand he writes you letters, Betsy-babes. Perhaps we could have a peek at some of them, just a little sneaky look. I think there are lots of people who'd be interested."

The bed creaked as Louise got up, then the other invaders rose. "Now I'm going to put this alarm clock very gently on the floor, because I don't want to break anything. But the rest of this junk on your trunk we'll just get rid of."

As my books were swept to the floor, I leapt from the bed. "Don't you touch my trunk, Louise, don't you dare."

"Pin her down, girls. Hey Betsy-babes, keep it down to a dull roar. We don't want to have to get rough."

I felt hands on my shoulders pushing me on the bed. I wouldn't fight. I'd learned not to from that wiry boy in fifth grade. But Louise had the top of my trunk open—I could see now that my eyes were accustomed to the dark. I'd say anything to keep her out of there.

"Panther, please. Come on, have pity. That's my private business in there. You wouldn't like it if someone did this to you."

Louise said nothing. She dug through the first layer of uniforms. I knew the letters and clippings were in my box, on the top, and that any second Louise would find them.

"You've probably got a packet tied with a nice pink ribbon and buried them deep. I'll find them. Oh lover boy, where are you?"

Maybe, just maybe Louise might pass by the letter

box. As my shirts were pulled from the trunk, I heard it plop softly on the floor. Louise kept digging.

"Come on, let's stop her," I begged the cabin. "Help me."

No one moved. Even Worm was too scared to help.

I grabbed the arm reaching in my trunk, but Louise shook me off. "I guess you don't understand. I want those letters."

I watched things fly from the trunk—underwear, pajamas, tennis shoes, the thin-heeled silver shoes.

Louise stood up. She bent and picked up a shoe by its strap. "Oh boy. Now I'd like to know what you're doing with a pair of shoes like this?"

My face burned.

"Hey! You weren't planning to wear these in the contest tomorrow, were you?"

My face burned hotter.

"Ooowee girls, I think we've found out one of Betsy-babes's little secrets, yes indeedy. But you got it all wrong, honey. These are classy shoes, they're for the *Beauty* Contest. In case you hadn't heard, you're in the *Ugly* Contest."

I was going to have to take this abuse. My treasure was too near, too dangerous. I wouldn't say a word, I'd take the humiliation. Let them have the shoes. And let them have rotten, stupid Duke. It would be horrible, but I'd live. Now Louise pawed through the trunk like a dog snuffling a meaty bone. She must be near the mustard sweater—anything, anything to get her out of there.

"*Okay. Stop.* I'll give you the letters. You can have them. I'll show you where they are."

But Louise's hand still drilled through the trunk,

her flashlight peering under every piece of clothing. She shook out a sweatshirt and hurled it on the floor. The mustard sweater would be next.

"I said stop! I'll get the letters," I brayed.

Too late. Louise had spied the gleam of something gold, of buried treasure.

"Oh my God," she said respectfully. She fell to her knees in front of the near empty trunk. "Oh my God," she repeated. "You're not going to believe your eyeballs. Come here, everyone."

Again the Fivers did not move. The Caw Caw Taws came around and looked over Louise's shoulder into the trunk.

"Well I'll be."

"You're kidding. You've got to be kidding."

I felt the heat in my face boil over and streams as scalding as molten lava run down my cheeks. My precious treasure trove. My victories. My secret.

"Get on over here Cabin Five, you've got to look at this. Wow. To think you dummies have been in the same cabin with *this* all summer."

I heard my cabinmates leave their beds and reluctantly shuffle over. I knew they were still frightened. Didn't they know that it was all finished, nothing else could happen? Didn't they realize this was the bottom, the end?

Two Caw Caw Taws stood shining their beam into the trunk, steady as miners' lights. Dede approached cautiously and peered over the edge, keeping her distance, as though she was expecting a trunk full of snakes. I heard her gasp.

Dede moved aside and Jolee took her place. The

other Fivers lined up behind her as though to view an embalmed corpse.

"Who would've thought it?" Anna asked softly. She sounded awed, yet a little mournful.

"Boy, that's something else," Jolee added.

"You bet it is," Louise crowed. She'd started the strange, thumping war dance again.

Stinging tears fell down my face and backed up inside my throat. They closed me off from the girls, from the room, from the darkness of my own secrets. I didn't have to listen, just feel the pain inside and out.

"I think we've got some questions we'd like to ask," Louise said, stepping in front of the trunk again. "I mean things look pretty suspicious to me."

I didn't care what they asked, I'd tell them whatever. There was no point to my secret anymore, no point to anything. My cabinmates had crept back to their beds; the room was as quiet as the night outside.

Louise cleared her throat. "What we need is a court of inquiry."

"We don't need a damn thing more from you." It was Worm.

"I *said* we need a court of inquiry. So where'd you get all this stuff?"

That was my treasure Louise was calling "stuff." Too late to correct her. I had no voice anyway.

"No answers, huh?"

"She doesn't have to say one word to you." Worm again.

"No answers means guilty. You stole it, didn't you? You stole it from your own cabinmates!"

"Wait a minute here," Anna said. "I've never been able to keep candy long enough to get it stolen! She hasn't taken anything from me, and that's for sure."

"I certainly haven't noticed anything missing," Julia added.

"I've never stolen anything in my life," I croaked, and gasped a huge sob as I remembered—Miss Mack's candies.

"Okay, let's hear it. How did you get all these goodies?"

The only sound was my crying, growing louder, as though that could carry me away from all this. "Can't you tell?" I sobbed. "Don't any of you ever notice anything? Either you don't have eyes or I'm invisible." I heaved another huge sob that seemed to shake tears from inside. "Look at me. I lost a lot of weight this summer."

"I noticed *that*," Cammy said. "I'm sure everyone knows *that*."

"Then why didn't anyone say anything?" I cried.

"I don't know," Cammy shrugged. "It's just not the kind of thing I like to talk about. It kind of makes me nervous. I mean we all have our own weight problems."

"What do you mean, Cammy? How can you say that when you've been in the Beauty Contest? And no one else in this cabin has had to diet."

"Get ahold of reality," Jolee said. "I'm always trying to lose five pounds. That's been going on for years."

"Everyone I know is on a diet," Wanda said. "That includes me."

"I've been worried you were getting anorexic," Worm added quietly.

"So how'd you get all that candy?" Anna asked.

"I saved it," I yelled. "I never ate one single candy bar all summer."

"Simmer down there, Betsy-babes," Louise hissed. "We're going to have that patrol here any minute."

"You know it, Panther," a Caw Caw Taw said as she eased toward the door. "I itch under this stocking anyway. Let's get out of here."

"Check. Let's blow it. Where's a bag?"

Again the cabin was silent.

"Come on now, someone give me a bag. You don't think we're going to let all this loot just sit here? Come on, cough it up or we'll have to do someone else's trunk."

I heard a rustling, then Louise had a paper bag.

"Boy, it's hard to believe she saved all this." Louise showered candy through her hands. "It's all here, the whole summer. Even the chocolates Miss Mack gives out. Here's one all mashed up, glued to the bottom of her trunk. Remember how she gives you one when she first meets you?"

"I thought she'd put a turd in my hand," snorted a Caw Caw Taw.

Louise scooped up double handfuls of treasure and plopped it in the bag. "Hey, you didn't want this anyway, Betsy-babes." Now her voice seemed nervous. "We're doing you a favor after all."

"Hurry Panther. I don't want to get caught."

Louise stood in the doorway, her face twisted under the stocking.

If there is really a Land Where All Wishes Are Granted, let Louise's face stay like that forever, I prayed.

" 'Bye girls. You've been real sports. The Caw Caw Taws would like to express their appreciation and say thanks for your hospitality. Here's a little party favor."

On each bed she threw one of my candy bars.

"Catch you on the flip side." The door slammed.

"What about the panties?" asked a Caw Caw Taw going down the steps.

"Next year."

There wasn't much to say inside Cabin Five.

Worm was by my side. "I'll help you fold up your clothes," she offered.

The girls held flashlights while I picked up the wrinkled clothing, piling it on the bed. I found the mustard sweater, and the letter box with Duke untouched. A last, stray tear of humiliation straggled down my face.

Jolee came to my trunk then, and laid a Mr. Goodbar in the bottom. Wanda put in a Tootsie Roll. Quietly, my cabinmates gave back the remnants of my treasure.

I couldn't sleep. Exhaustion left me numb though, and in the moments I almost drifted off I saw Wishing Boats, bobbing black on Lake Sunset over the tendrils of slimy lake weeds. The sails were photographs, muddy, dark, but still recognizable. Miss Mack. Louise. Mother—what was Mother doing there? The wind came up, a whirlpool sucked open in the lake, and the little boats were reeling, whirling down to the weeds. Round and round, down farther and farther to the Land Where All Wishes Are Granted.

13 ✳ *Thinking Ugly*

The day sparkled for the contest. Little jewel lights bounced off the crest of lake ripples, winked, disappeared, and twinkled again. Wavelets rolled to the shore like strings of pearls. Cutting firmly out into Lake Sunset was the big dock—not the shaky dips dock, but a boulevard of planks, an unshakable pier. Around it was the swimming area, and on it the spring diving board and the high dive platform.

"Okay. What are they doing now?"

"They're sweeping the dock, starting at the end."

Worm and I crept along the beach-fringe of birches, spying on the set-up crew. My secret task—the one that had me up at dawn—was completed. When Worm found me on the beach, trying to scope out this contest, she pulled me off into the woods. "Don't let them see you. You don't want to get caught at anything," she warned. "Lie low. I'll do the looking."

"Why do they have to sweep the dock?" I asked.

"What would happen if a tiny grain of sand rolled

under a Bathing Beauty's shoe? Can you imagine her skidding across the dock?"

I had to bury my giggle in my hand.

"They're almost finished now—but they're inching down the dock. Man, do they work slowly. Okay. Done. Now they're heading toward the Counselors' Den."

Worm and I followed, slinking around trees and crouching behind low blueberry bushes. I dared a look when I heard the set-up crew give a five-knock rap. The door of the little shack was cracked warily and shut quickly again, forcing out a waft of smoke.

"Can you imagine anyone actually taking that stuff in their lungs?" Worm whispered.

The door opened, and a hand passed out two folded aluminum chairs with webbed seats. The crew returned to the dock.

"They're brushing sand from their feet," Worm reported. "Now they're carrying the chairs to the dock end."

"Those have to be thrones for Dusty and Miss Mack."

"Duck lower," Worm whispered. "They're coming this way. Wait—no—they've turned into the bath house. Listen, I can hear them sweeping it. I'll bet they're cleaning the full-length mirror, too."

"That's got to be the Bathing Beauties' dressing room."

"You're right. Look. They're coming out and moving down the beach. They've got rakes now. They're going to try and clean up the icky weed heaps."

All summer, shore patrol had waded waist deep into the slimy, grasping weeds, pulling until the roots gave up the mud, so the swimming area would be clear. They heaved them in dripping handfuls into a rowboat, then forked them into mounds on the beach. Dusty carted off old heaps in the pickup truck, and the shore patrol made new ones. Now, piled too high, the weed heaps flopped over and the crew pounded them back into snarled black cones.

"Hey, they're moving into the boat shed," Worm reported.

I peeked up to see the boat shed, at the edge of the outermost weed heap. Open on four sides, sand for a floor, it sheltered racks of canoes and night birds roosting in its rafters. I watched the crew nail up an army blanket over the end facing the dock.

"I'll bet ten million dollars that's the Bathing Uglies' dressing room," I said to Worm.

I was no longer interested in Beauty. I didn't care about Beauty's dressing room or swept boardwalk. I only wanted to know where the Uglies would be. I had plans for this contest.

The boathouse was perfect for a dressing room. Those Bathing Beauties all had to change together in one room like a cut-rate department store. But the Uglies had canoe racks that made little cubicles. If I got there early I could seize the end one. I'd nail up my own blanket and be private. It wouldn't be like Mother's dressing room with a flounce-skirted dressing table and triple mirror, but it would be mine.

"Okay Worm. I think I have the picture now."

"I'm not sure I understand what this picture's all about," Worm said, her forehead scrunched and puzzled.

"Ugly. That's all I can tell you now. But thanks for

helping. You're a real friend, you know. Let's go to lunch. I think we're having pizza."

And pizza it was, scored into big wedges. I vowed not to worry about this food business again—there were larger issues. So what if my bathing suit fit a little tight this afternoon? What difference did that make? I planned to eat when I was hungry and enjoy it. I maneuvered a mozzarella cheese string back onto my pizza slice.

"I still consider myself a vegetarian, but I've gotten pretty fond of sausage, especially on pizza," Worm said. "I wonder how my mom will deal with that when I get home? She'll probably put me on a blood purification program. Boiled nettles or something."

Wanda sat on my other side. "I adore pizza," she told me in a confidential voice, "but I find it lasts longer if you use a knife and fork. And between us, you notice I never touch the outside crust. Way, way too fattening."

That was one of the best parts—the crunchy end of the pizza. All summer I'd been watching Wanda put a tomato slice and a shredded piece of bacon between two lettuce leaves and call it a BLT. No mayonnaise, no triple layer of bread. And I thought that must be how she liked it, for some crazy reason. Diets. They'd all been on diets.

Jolee—slender as could be—ate spaghetti in a most incredible way. One by one she ran each strand through her mouth, sucked it clean, then returned white shoelaces to her plate.

Not me.

I picked up an Eskimo Pie from the tray by the

door, then bit through a crackly chocolate coating, rolling the ice cream in my mouth. The inside dissolved until only the wood stick was left to lick.

On the way up the hill, the horrible posture perfect song spun through my head, the end catching like a scratched record.

"Do not slump, do not slump. . . .
　　Hide that hump,
　　Hide that hump."

Oh yes, I thought, there's more hiding around here than a hump, and I'm not going to be a part of it any longer. This Bathing Ugly would hump that hide, that thick hide. I would, and they'd remember it.

Rest hour in the cabin. Anna played solitaire cross-legged on the bed. Cammy touched-up her fingernails. Wanda's head was re-curled and tied up in the net again. Cammy sat facing her pillow, back to everyone. Debbie Sue lay on her bed, arm over her eyes, mouth open, as though asleep. I didn't think she was.

I opened to the sports section of the newspaper from habit, but there was no news of Duke today. Excellent. The first favorable omen. Louise hadn't found his letters last night, and now they were all decaying in the pit of the Brown. Duke was gone from my life forever. I'd paid for that stupid idea, in self-respect. I hoped I'd never hear another thing about him.

I sensed the cabin's tension in the noisy rustling of my newspaper and the slap of Anna's cards. Dede came in and lay down, chewing her Eskimo Pie stick, splintering it, gnashing the tip. All of us could only think of one thing: The Contest.

It was too much for everyone. It hadn't happened yet and already we were tired of it. We circled it with an edgy boredom. In a few hours we'd judge and be judged. We were exhausted from all the preparations and anxious to be rid of the event.

Cammy sighed loudly.

Anna's cards clicked and whirred as she shuffled.

Debbie Sue began to snore.

I turned on my side and stared through the screen at the pine trees, squinting my eyes to make them blurry.

Screen doors slammed and a far-away voice laughed while the pines shook back into focus.

"Let's *go* Cabin Fivers!" Like a firecracker thrown in the cabin, Debbie Sue exploded. She gave the touchdown split-leap of the Iowa High Flingers. She jumped around the beds, poking and pulling at each of us.

"Come on, get up! This is it! The big day! The big hour!" She tugged at my arms, then messed the top of my head so it looked like a milk shake.

Debbie Sue strutted over to Wanda, knees prancing waist high, arms making big air circles as though they had pom-poms for hands. "Here we go, kid, whoopee! You are going to be the most splendiferous Bathing

Beauty there ever was! Come on now, we'll do your comb-out down in the Beauties' dressing room."

"What should I do, Debbie Sue?" Julia laced her shoes and tucked in her shirt, standing ready.

"Julia, you take the make-up tray. Make sure everything's there. Don't forget Cammy's Wet and Wild lip gloss."

Julia swooped up the tray of creams, tubes, small tan bottles, lipstick cylinders. She balanced it on her palms, propped open the screen door with her foot and slid out.

"Who has the ribbon?"

"I do."

"Good. Don't fold it. Keep it perfect."

Dawn left with the glittery name banner looped down between her forearms.

"Where's the bathing suit?"

"Here."

"Who has the shoes?"

"I do."

"Hairbrush and comb? Clips, headband, hair-spray?"

Debbie Sue braced her clipboard on her hip and checked off each camper as she went out. Around her neck hung her whistle on its braided lariat. Debbie Sue looked normal, ready for swimming lesson, just the way I saw her on the beach every day. But today wasn't normal.

They'd all left but Debbie Sue, and she'd be going to the dressing room any second. I opened my trunk, guarding it from old habit, like a basketball player, arms and legs spread. The silver shoes were on top, their delicate straps and slim heels waiting for my feet, waiting for me to walk down the boardwalk, no matter what nasty remarks Louise had made. I heard Debbie Sue move from the door, but not in the right direction. She was coming toward me. I slammed down the trunk lid.

"Hurry up Bets, we've got to get down there. Aren't you ready yet?"

"I'll be right along. You go ahead."

"Hey, what are you doing, anyway?" Her attention was full on me now. She looked long at the treasure chest, then shifted her eyes to my face, with the same stare she'd used when I'd read Duke's letter to the cabin. She stepped closer. "What's going on here? Is there something funny about that trunk?"

"Not a thing, Debbie Sue. Why? Have you heard anything funny?"

"Anything funny about what?"

"About last night."

She said nothing. I felt the ghosts of Louise and the Caw Caw Taws stomp through the cabin.

"You're a strange kid sometimes," she said at last. "Why are you looking so guilty?"

I did look guilty, I knew it, but I had to look at the floor to keep her from seeing the tears that started behind my eyes.

"Come on, Bets, lighten up. Look, I didn't hear anything. But if you guys want to have a party, no one's going to squeal on you. And you can keep whatever you want in your trunk."

She didn't know what had happened—or she didn't know it all. My treasure might have been stolen, but it didn't have to affect the rest of my life.

"Oh that's not the problem, Debbie Sue—in fact there isn't any problem. But you're right, I do have something in my trunk."

I lifted the top a few inches, poked my arm under, and waggled my fingers until I hooked the shoe straps. The silver sandals came heaving out. I held them up, the prize catch.

Debbie Sue smiled. "Absolutely great idea, Bets."

"You really think so?"

"Sure. You're a riot. You'll wear those in the Ugly Contest? Too hysterical for words. Now what else do you have for a costume? A funny hat? Did you look in the dramatics box? Hey wait a minute—I've got something else."

She went down on hands and knees, pulling out boxes from under her bed. From one she drew a long see-through chartreuse scarf, filmy, something to fill in a sweater at the throat, or softly line a spring coat.

"Look Bets, you could tie your hair up in this." She plastered down her own blonde hair, turning it brassy green through the scarf. "Or wear it like a ribbon." She folded it and strapped it across her shoulder to her waist.

"Absolutely great idea, Debbie Sue." Those had been her words. I tied the scarf into a big puffed bow, holding it to my wrist as though it were a tender green orchid and I was going to a fraternity dance rather than an Ugly Contest.

She laughed. "Good luck, kid." Giving my cheek a tweak, she left.

I set the scarf on her bed. Slowly I followed with my own body. A light body? A heavy body? I didn't know anymore.

I did know I didn't want this stupid scarf. And the silver shoes were ordinary, tacky, as Mother would say. There was nothing original about them. Why would it be funny if I wore them? Why would girls laugh at my silver shoes and not at Wanda's satin ones? What would make the chartreuse scarf funny on me but not on Debbie Sue?

It was all wrong. Not my idea of Bathing Ugly at all. Once again I'd let myself be fooled when I knew the truth. I knew exactly what must happen. After last night there was nothing left to risk.

I tied the shoes in the scarf like hobo possessions and left them on Debbie's bed. And no one was going to see me out there in my seersucker bathing suit. I looked over the Fiver's suits hooked on the wall and picked a bright red tank suit. A small one.

I stuck my leg through the top, threading it out the leg hole. As I pulled the suit up, it felt snug by the knee, then squeezed my thigh tighter, higher. Hopping one-legged, I pushed in the other leg. I tugged and stretched until the suit was anchored between my legs and pulled across my behind. Then I dove into the arm loops, bent over, and secured them on my shoulders. I straightened slowly, knowing it was a real test for the seams. The nylon stretched full of me. But it held.

I was, all of me, in a small red tank suit. My plaid bathrobe would cover it; I tied it tightly. In its pocket was my toothpaste that wormed out green chlorophyll stripes. That was going to come in handy. By the door I picked up black rubber swim fins. Never mind the snorkel and mask—the fins were all I needed.

I stood on the steps for a second looking down Cabin Hill, almost to Lake Sunset. Something important waited for me there. The Land Where All Wishes Are Granted. Maybe I should have doubled my B-vitamins as Worm had suggested. Instead I closed my eyes and breathed deeply through my nose. My nerve felt steady. Bathing Ugly was on her way.

14 ✳ Bathing Ugly

Sunny Days campers buzzed on the edge of the beach, their calls and chatter like a high-pitched mosquito hum. Some darted around the Beauties' dressing room or ran back to cabins for more hairspray or another box of cotton puffs. Girls without errands quickly grabbed the front-line viewing spots next to the lake.

As I looked down the sand I saw them sitting with rounded backs and hunched shoulders, knees scooped close to their chests like insects ready to spring. Beyond them, high and solid over Lake Sunset, was the dock walkway with aluminum thrones waiting at the end for Miss Mack and Dusty.

The boathouse dressing room was busy too. Uglies were making Ugly. Cabinmates helped. I heard giggles and yelps behind the next canoe rack.

"My God, you're a howl!"

"You've got this one sewed up, I'm telling you."

Worm ducked under my blanket door. "Let me give you a hand getting ready, Bets."

"No Worm, you go sit with the Fivers. Work them up into a good cheering section for me."

"But that's not where I want to be."

"I know, and I appreciate it. But—" I put my hand on my heart and rolled up my eyes—"this is something I have to do alone."

"All right Lieutenant," she said, saluting. "In that case, give 'em hell."

I counted thirty Mississippi to give Worm time to get to the dock, then peeked over my tent flap blanket. Seeing no one at that end of the boathouse, I slipped outside.

On the beach, out of reach of the wavelets were the heaps of seaweed yanked from the lake. Like the crusts of huge, dark bread loaves, the tops were black and dried—the insides an uncooked, slimy green of snarled weeds. I grabbed for the middle and jerked out a handful, loading up my arm. The deeper I reached, the more dank and rotted the seaweed smelled. The last fistful felt like well-chewed celery.

I carried a big load of the sloppy weeds to the boathouse, their stinking tendrils trailing after me, mopping at the sand. I dropped them in my dressing room. They took over my air.

I was almost ready to start—except for one last secret thing to retrieve for my Ugliness. But I knew where it was and when to get it.

Squatting by the lake, I washed the jelly-like weed residue from my arms and shivered with relief when I was clean.

Down the beach the entire camp had gathered. All of them: my rivals, my cabinmates, my friends, my tormenters. The girls crammed close to the dock, piling up like snowdrifts on the beach in their Sunday white shorts. I leaned against the canoe shed and watched the proceedings as comfortably as if seeing a parade from my own front porch.

Miss Mack marched up the dock, shoulders back, chest puffed out, knees stiff. I was too far away to see her expression, but I imagined her lips clamped back so tightly they outlined her teeth and gums. She put the big cone megaphone to her mouth; her left arm flew up in the air and stopped at an angle that meant silence. Campers scrambled to stand at attention. Her arm sailed out, then from the megaphone came her high, scratchy voice backed by the campers' chorus a quarter beat behind.

> "Oh we're from Sunny Days, Sunny Days!
> Oh it's simply grand, girls on every hand
> Oh we're from Sunny Days, Sunny Days!
> That's where we have our fun."

I stood listening to the song finish as though it were the Star Spangled Banner.

"This is, I am pleased to announce, the thirty-fourth annual Camp Sunny Days Bathing Beauty and Bathing Ugly Contest." Applause and whistles.

"And now," screeched the tinny, amplified voice that was Miss Mack, "I'd like to introduce King Neptune, who will this day choose the Fairest of the Land to reign over his court!"

King Neptune?

"Ladies, let's welcome the Marine Monarch of the Sea! His Oceanic Majesty!"

There wasn't much doubt that the old man who swaggered out onto the dock was Dusty. The white beard that hung to Neptune's knees looked salvaged from an old Santa Claus costume, and the pitchfork was the same one that worked away at weed heaps. Under the beard was a bathrobe that came almost to his ankles—perhaps inherited from a taller, larger man. The upper part of his face looked red as his hair. I heard clop-clop applause from the campers.

"Girls, girls. May I have your attention." It was Miss Mack again. "Now it's time to look at our Sunny Days Beauties, the loveliest, comeliest girls we have." Her right hand clamped to her chest the way it did when she said the Pledge of Allegiance. "One of these girls will be our Miss Bathing Beauty, so posture perfect ladies, and bring on the contestant from Cabin Number One."

Up the dock steps came a Beauty. As she moved onto the walkway she stopped and turned so the campers could see her from all sides. This Beauty was radiant, her color blushing, her smile self-assured and never failing. Her glossy hair was fluffy on her shoulders. Her smooth, fluid body flowed with grace from breasts to waist to hips. Her legs were the perfect length, the perfect size, and the high heels that arched her ankles made them seem delicate as a fawn's.

With longing that made me want to burst apart on the beach, I watched the Beauty glide out to Miss

Mack and Neptune-Dusty. She pivoted twice, jutting out her hip and smiling. Not even if I threw sand in everyone's face and pushed that Beauty off the dock was there any way I could take her place. Ever. There was no Good Witch of Oz. I could only be myself, and be more of myself.

The Beauties kept coming. Everyone applauded, but I sensed a politeness in it. Envy in every hand clap. Beauties strode down the walkway, their ribbons glittering in the late afternoon sun, scattering reflections on their subjects. None of them looked exhausted from a sleepless night. There were no Band-Aids on their legs. They didn't have zits ready to explode on their foreheads.

When they finished, the Beauties didn't sit in the sand with the others; they stood in a line that curved out like a small rainbow across the beach.

I went back inside my dressing room. It was time to begin. From my robe pocket I took my toothpaste, plump and full. I flopped back my head and looked up at the rafters. I squeezed ribbons of toothpaste on my forehead.

"You've done a fine job ladies. I'm proud of you all," came Miss Mack's megaphone voice through my blanket. She was talking to the Beauties.

Toothpaste came out in long worms, crisscrossed my forehead, looped my cheeks. It felt cold and stung a little. I coiled it near my chin.

"Now, as we do every year, we'll go on to Bathing Ugly. And all the counselors tell me this year's contestants are the best and funniest ever."

I looped the green and white toothpaste up and down my nose.

"So let's get going with Cabin Number One!"

I needed no mirror. As I ringed my eyes with toothpaste I felt it settle into my eyebrows and pucker the tender skin on my cheeks.

There was quiet in the dressing room as the first Ugly went out.

What did it feel like being stared at? Was it hard to take the first steps out of the boat house? Then I heard whoops, cheers, clapping from the audience.

Braced against a canoe, I pushed my foot into a black webbed swim fin. My toes were cramped against the hard rubber. I looked down my legs at them and thought I looked like a prehistoric giant bird. Or a little like Miss Mack in her high-tops.

Down the beach applause faded.

"Very good, girls. Now let's have our contestant from Cabin Number Two, please." Miss Mack's mechanical voice ended in a squawk.

From my personal, stinking pile, I took a handful of weeds and slid them in my red tank suit between my breasts. I shuddered when I jammed those jelly-slime weeds next to my body—as though they could grow into me. They knotted up and spilled out like a coarse tangle of chest hair. I grabbed more. I knew I couldn't back out now—this was the moment. I stuffed them under my straps, dark evil-smelling shoulder pads. Tight as an elastic band, my suit pressed the weeds under my arm into a soggy armpit-pelt.

The megaphone cut the distance from the dock to the boathouse. "Cabin Number Three, please."

"*Go* Patty, *go. Go* Patty, *go!*" her cabin cheered.

I had to work faster. I anchored seaweed at my

hip to stream down like a mucky hula skirt. I stuffed seaweed in my crotch to dribble down my inside thighs. My secret fear. I was lumpier and bumpier inside my suit than I'd been at my fattest.

There was clapping and laughing in the boat shed as another Ugly went out. "Cabin Number Four," Miss Mack called.

As I picked up the last glob of seaweed, a big cow leech, spotted and yellow, fell onto the sand. I jumped back and almost screamed. But as I looked down at it, I knew that bloodsucker had to be part of me. Trembling, I picked the disgusting thing up and held it to my forehead until I felt it attach to my skin. That was it—I now had what that airline stewardess didn't have. A special eye.

I crammed the seaweed on my head. A hideous wig of tangled snakes, wet and oozing, clung to my skull. It was so heavy I could hardly walk. My neck was clammy cold and stiff already. Miss Mack would call me next, sure as my turn always came at the weigh-ins. I left my boathouse dressing room, slid under the blanket with bent knees, balancing my crop of hair carefully as any Beauty. I guided my clumsy platypus flippers onto the sand.

This morning at dawn, before Worm discovered me on the beach, I'd found a washed-up, rotting fish head. I had buried it next to the weed mound. I feared the set-up crew would find it, for the awful stench filtered even through the weed tombstone I'd made. But this time no one stole my treasure.

I scraped at the sand. "Cabin Number Five, please," sounded like a fog horn.

I picked up the fish head. The soft decaying flesh

was in my hand. Its round eye, circled with white, stared up at my special eye.

I walked toward the dock slowly—slowly, give them lots of time, take it slow, knees pointed out, back rounded like a troll a lifetime in the swamps. My arms were level at shoulder height, making an altar for my fish head. I stared straight ahead, concentrated on walking low and slow, balancing my weed wig.

I heard no laughter, no clapping from my fellow campers on the beach. Girls scooted back on the sand as I passed.

"Phew," one said. That was all.

My flipper was at the dock steps. I mounted them with legs frogged out, slapping at the steps with my webbing. One. Two. Three. Then I was on the dock, the long walk to Miss Mack and His Oceanic Majesty.

I began to groan, not loudly, but low in my throat, drawn out. I slowed down even more; this had to take a long time, though my heart was beating fast in my ears, urging me on more quickly. Slow. Sweat mixed with the ooze dripping down my chest and back. The toothpaste began to soften on my face. I felt it slip a little on my forehead.

My flippers thudded against the dock planks. I brought them down smack! as hard as I could, making an echo between the dock and the water. My shoulders were exhausted from keeping my arms out, and only my locked elbows seemed to keep them up. Smack! Nightmare sleep walker. Think Ugly, Ugly. The green toothpaste bit into my skin, slipping and stinging. I saw the fish at eye level, its pink scales chopped by a straight cut. Slowly, slowly.

I was halfway there. I imagined myself an unwrapped mummy. Through the toothpaste that threatened my eyelids, I could see Miss Mack's face. She was not smiling. She glowered. I felt a fierceness come over me and center in my eyes. I held Miss Mack's eyes as I slapped and dragged toward her.

I switched to Dusty's eyes, his glass one like the bulging round eye of the fish, never moving. Back to Miss Mack. They sat at the end of the dock in thrones, those judges, gripping their chairs as though they expected a high wind to blow them off the dock.

I was there, a ghost from a watery grave. I bowed from the waist, holding up my Medusa head, arms out. Looking up under toothpaste eyebrows, I offered Miss Mack my fish head. It was right under her nose.

She tilted back her head and shook it from side to side, jowls flapping, wrinkle chasing wrinkle. "Take that thing away," she yelled.

Dusty jumped his chair back dangerously close to the edge of the dock.

"You've gone too far," Miss Mack shrieked. "Really, how distasteful. I'm surprised at you. I expected better things."

Oh you did, huh? Well so did I.

I straightened and, dignified, turned my back on Miss Mack and King Neptune and started to waddle my chicken walk down the dock. Everything was melting, mixing painfully, eating into my skin. I hurt all over. The fish head stank. *Take that thing away,* Miss Mack had said.

But I was right there at the ladder that led up to the high dive. Before I knew what I'd done, I let my fish head slide to the dock, grabbed the railing, and climbed the ladder, toes pointed to angle my flippers down the rungs. And then I was there, high, high in the sky, standing almost in the clouds. I went straight out to the end of the board. There was one dizzy second before I was in the air, but it was elation, not fear. On my flight I grabbed my knees and tucked my head. The water closed over me and I felt myself sinking down to the weeds.

A push with the flippers and I shot to the top, bursting through the surface, gulping air. I heard big waves crashing, then I realized they were roars. It was Camp Sunny Days cheering for me. I rolled over on my back and listened. It went on and on. A chant started up, "Go Betsy, go! Go Betsy, go!"

As I started paddling to shore, I saw someone swimming toward me, arms stroking hard, head out of the water. Although her hair was plastered to her neck, it took me only a second to realize it was Lolly Sharp.

"You did it! You did it!" she yelled as she came closer. "You really did show them a thing or two. Oh Bets, you're fantastic!"

We were treading water, grinning at each other. I turned and saw Miss Mack and King Neptune standing on the dock, glaring in our direction.

"Look. Your head-weeds are floating over there. I'll go get them." Lolly swam to the little island of weeds—my wig—that had left me when I hit the water. "Do you think you can swim with them? I want you to be perfect when you reach land."

I dunked down and came up under my weeds. As I settled them on my head, my hand passed over my forehead and recoiled. The cow leech was still there. It took salt or a burning match to get rid of a leech. As Lolly and I began swimming to shore, I could hear the whole camp still booming, *"Go Betsy, go! Go Betsy, go!"*

Lolly helped me out of the water, and I stood there dripping a mixture of water, weeds, and diluted toothpaste. The camp yelped with laughter. They clapped and stomped. Lolly grabbed my hand and held it high—not the private clench of buddy check, but a public show of friendship and victory.

I sat down on the beach to watch the rest of my fellow Uglies finish the contest. They were dressed in floppy hats and funny old-time bathing suits like the ones Beauties wore in Miss Mack's pictures. There was an Ugly with waxed buck teeth; there was another in argyle socks and high heels. One had huge pillow rolls under an outsized yellow sun dress.

Was that what I'd looked like fat? I tried to remember that this was make-fun. My fat had been real. I couldn't forget that these Uglies were friends who'd been chosen especially for this job because of their plainness or skinniness or pimples or bad teeth. Maybe the other campers felt the same way, for though there was applause for the remaining Uglies, it sounded hesitant, a little sheepish.

I looked through the crowd for Debbie Sue but I couldn't find her. Instead I saw Miss Mack, striding down the dock, megaphone in her hand. The Marine Monarch of the Sea trailed after her, his beard peeled off one side of his face.

"Girls! Girls! Girls! Attention now. We've had a

great deal more excitement this afternoon than we should have had. Calm down immediately."

So she did know something was different this year.

"The judges have conferred, and we're now going to crown our Bathing Beauty. Girls, gather in a semicircle please."

She turned to the Bathing Beauties. "You've done a splendid job, ladies. I'm proud of you all." The enthusiasm that had led Camp Sunny Days into its thirty-fourth year was in her voice. "Good straight backs, fine girls! How I wish you all could win. Ah, uncorrupted flowering of womanhood."

What on earth could Miss Mack be talking about? Even the Beauties looked at each other nervously.

"There's only one winner, but remember dear girls, someday it may be you. And remember also—keep this closely in your hearts—if you are not the winner, you are a runner-up. Now King Neptune, will you hand me the card with the winner's name?"

Beaming, Dusty fumbled in his bathrobe pocket.

"And the winner is! Marlinda Porter, from Cabin Two. You are our new Bathing Beauty."

Marlinda stepped out, a blush spreading from her face down into her bathing suit. Her eyes had misted over and her mouth corners quivered, but as I looked down the line of unchosen, not-quite-up-to-snuff Beauties, I saw theirs had too. They must be aching to know what their flaws were. I realized they now probably thought there was something wrong with them—like having an extra pound or two. I saw Wanda's stricken face and wanted to comfort her.

"Here comes King Neptune with the crown," Miss Mack crowed.

Dusty had left her side and reappeared now with a familiar, white satin, tufted box. I had no trouble seeing two distinct, brown smudges on the lid. He held the box out to Miss Mack, and she extracted a flat, foil-covered paper crown that could have been made of chocolate wrappers.

"Kneel, Marlinda."

Marlinda hesitated. She looked back at the would-be Beauty Queens for confirmation. Then she sank to the sand on her knees, her eyes level with Miss Mack's thighs. Miss Mack held the crown high, her arms straight up and trembling a little, as though making an offering to the gods of Lake Sunset.

"The words of Elizabeth Barrett Browning," she said to the sky.

"The beautiful seems right
    By force of Beauty, and the feeble wrong
    By force of weakness."

She placed the crown on Bathing Beauty.

Had I heard right? If so, Miss Mack had it all wrong. Feeble and weak—never.

Miss Mack turned to the Uglies. It was our turn now.

My face burned, my scalp itched. The seaweed clots were gross inside my suit. I blotted clammy drops of seepage from my face with the back of my hand, avoiding my special eye. My palms smelled. The mop of seaweed on my head made an ache that traveled down my neck. A breeze came up, making waves glitter like crowns. I shivered, a very cold sea monster.

More than anything I wanted that fish head back, for I knew it gave me power and strength. And then I knew I was in the Land Where All Wishes Are Granted, for from the corner of my eye I saw Worm coming off the dock, with the fish head in her hand. She stood next to me, looked straight at Miss Mack, and proudly gave it to me.

Now I was able to put all the fierceness I felt on the dock back in my eyes. I stooped my shoulders and my spine curved forward; I folded again into my crouch. Low, almost squat, holding out the fish head, I was in ready position.

"We have a winner in the Ugly contest too."

Was I mistaken, or had her voice become flat, chilly as the stiff breeze? She looked around her audience, but passed her eyes over the heads of the Uglies.

"Our new Bathing Ugly is," she began tonelessly, "as you've probably guessed, Betsy Sherman, from Cabin Five." The last words sounded bitter.

"Atta girl."

"Congrats, Bets!"

"You did it for all of us," one of the Uglies said. "That Ugly Contest will never be the same again."

The Fivers moved around me in a respectful circle.

"I knew you'd do it, Bets," Julia said.

"You were wonderful," Wanda said. I could tell she'd been crying.

"It should have been you, too," I said. Although I thought it really didn't make any difference if you

won the contest or not when you're so pretty. But I
didn't tell her that. Probably it wouldn't have made
her feel any better.

"We'll have some time with that prize tonight, huh?"
Dede chortled. "Where do you collect those candy
bars, anyway?"

I knew what this win was for. Last night my treasure
had been stolen; tonight it would be given back. But
this time it would be free—something to celebrate,
not something to hide. I could share it. I didn't want
it all to myself. I didn't want all I wanted.

"Please ladies, quiet down. I have another announcement."

We were quiet, but in arrested motion as though
we were playing freeze.

"We will now begin the most exciting part of the
prize. Let's have the winners on the dock to circle
Lake Sunset. Dusty—King Neptune—get the patrol
boat. And I have my camera to photograph Beauty."

I unwound from my crouch at last, testing my
strained knees. I started back to the boathouse dressing room, shaking my head. I heard a flapping behind
me, then fingers grabbed my arm tightly as a bird of
prey.

"Where the heck are you going?" It was Louise.

"Back to the canoe shed." I shook off her hand.

"Dusty's getting the boat. What's wrong with you?
This is the chance of a lifetime! This is your chance
to make it!"

"Louise—I mean Panther—you would think so.
You're just the type. But keep on trying. Maybe next
year it can be you or another of the wonderful Caw
Caw Taws."

"Hey, we're thinking about letting you join."

"Shove it, Louise."

"Betsy?" Miss Mack called sharply. It was a command. I couldn't pretend I hadn't heard. "What's going on here? Aren't you going around the lake with Dusty?"

"No thank you, Miss Mack," I said politely. "I really don't want to do that." Life had been hard enough with a Duke. Who needed a King? I pulled the weed wig from my head, releasing a great rank odor. I wiped around my eyes with my knuckles.

Miss Mack shrugged her thin shoulders in a sharp, quick movement—the first time I'd seen them not held firmly back. I was sure no one had turned down the honor of riding with Neptune before. But if I could go too far once, I could go too far again.

"Of course not," Miss Mack said. "I'd want to take off that insane costume too." She turned away, as distinctly as I'd turned from her on the dock.

Something golden broke from the birch woods, flying toward me on the beach. It was Debbie Sue! Her blonde hair blew around her face, and she was running hard.

"Hey Bets!" she called. She was out of breath; that was all she could say. Then I saw she had her camera—she'd run all the way back to the cabin for her camera.

"Get that gorgeous wig back on," she gasped. "Oh this will knock them dead." She planted her legs firmly, but she was still winded and the camera at her eye moved up and down with her panting.

I smashed the weeds back on my head. My crown.

"Okay now, hold up your fish head."

That was the only excuse I needed. I put it next

to my cheek. Over Debbie Sue's shoulder I saw Miss Mack moving to the dock. Dusty had brought up the patrol boat, its Camp Sunny Days flag waving proudly from the stern. With his hand on the throttle he stood and gave his other hand to Marlinda, helped her into the wobbling boat.

How would she survive that cold, windy trip in her bathing suit, I wondered. No one had brought her a sweat shirt or blanket. It might spoil her looks.

I stood in front of the camera, staring into its lens while Debbie Sue peered through the view finder and wiggled the focus. I felt that fierceness come back into my eyes. I glared at the camera.

"That's it, kiddo. You're terrific. Hold it now!"